# THE
# SELECTED
# STORIES
## *of*
# GORDON
# LISH

# THE

# SELECTED

# STORIES

## *o f*

# GORDON

# LISH

*A Patrick Crean Book*

SOMERVILLE HOUSE PUBLISHING

TORONTO

CANADIAN CATALOGUING IN PUBLICATION DATA

LISH, GORDON
THE SELECTED STORIES OF GORDON LISH

"A PATRICK CREAN BOOK".
ISBN 1-895897-74-2

I. TITLE.

PS3562.I74S4  1996      813'.54      C96-931516-3

PRINTED IN CANADA

A PATRICK CREAN BOOK

PUBLISHED BY SOMERVILLE HOUSE PUBLISHING,
A DIVISION OF SOMERVILLE HOUSE BOOKS LIMITED,
3080 YONGE STREET, SUITE 5000, TORONTO, ONTARIO  M4N 3N1
INTERNET: SOMBOOKS@GOODMEDIA.COM
WEB: HTTP//WWW.GOODMEDIA.COM/SOMERVILLEHOUSE

SOMERVILLE HOUSE PUBLISHING ACKNOWLEDGES THE FINANCIAL
ASSISTANCE OF THE ONTARIO PUBLISHING CENTRE, THE ONTARIO
ARTS COUNCIL, THE ONTARIO DEVELOPMENT CORPORATION,
AND THE DEPARTMENT OF COMMUNICATIONS.

FOR JEN
FOR BEC
FOR ETH

FOR PEARL
FOR NINA SKY
FOR BORUS

FOR ILENE
FOR ANDREW
FOR FRED

FOR K.G. TRAKAS
FOR H. ROBERT BEARNOT
FOR JOHN G.H. OAKES

FOR DANA
FOR JODI
FOR ANDREOU
FOR KRUPP

AND FOR DELILLO, DELILLO, DELILLO

*A scruple in some occult relation to his feelings*
*results in this stress of reiteration,*
*its heavy stopping upon the prepositions*
*lest they resolve the matter prematurely*
*by accepting the offer of the noun.*

— DENIS DONOGHUE

# CONTENTS

———

# THE
# SELECTED
# STORIES
### *of*
# GORDON
# LISH

# THE DEATH

# OF ME

―――――

I WANTED TO BE AMAZING. I wanted to be so amazing. I had already been amazing up to a certain point. But I was tired of being at that point. I wanted to go past that point. I wanted to be more amazing than I had been up to that point. I wanted to do something which went beyond that point and which went beyond every other point and which people would look at and say that this was something which went beyond all other points and which no other boy would ever be able to go beyond, that I was the only boy who could, that I was the only one.

I was going to a day camp which was called the Peninsula Athletes Day Camp and which at the end of the summer had an all-campers, all-parents, all-sports field day which was made up of five different field events, and all of the campers had to take part in all five of all of the different field events, and I was the winner in all five of the five different field events, I was the winner in every single field event, I came in first place in every one of the five different field events—so that the head of the camp and the camp counselors and the other campers and the other mothers and the other fathers and my mother and my father all saw that I was the best camper in the Peninsula Athletes Day Camp, the best in the short run and the best in the long run and the best in the high jump and the best in the broad jump and the best in the event which the Peninsula Athletes Day Camp called the ball-throw, which was where you had to go up to a chalk line and then put your toe on the chalk line and not go over the chalk line and then throw the ball as far as you could throw.

I did.

I won.

It was 1944 and I was ten years old and I was better than all of the other boys at that camp and probably all of the boys every-where else.

I felt more wonderful than I had ever felt. I felt so thrilled with myself. I felt like God was whispering things to me inside of my head. I felt like God was asking me to have a special secret with him or to have a secret arrangement with him and that I had to keep listening to his secret recommendations to me inside of my head. I felt like God was telling me to realize that he had made me the most unusual member of the human race and that he was going to need me to be ready for him to go to work for him at any minute for him on whatever thing he said.

They gave me a piece of stiff cloth which was in the shape of a shield and which was in the camp colors and which had five blue stars on it. They said that I was the only boy ever to get a shield with as many as that many stars on it. They said that it was unheard-of for any boy ever to get as many as that many stars on it. But I could already feel that I was forgetting what it felt like to do something which would get you a shield with as many as that many stars on it. I could feel myself forgetting and I could feel everybody else forgetting, even my mother and father and God forgetting. It was just a little while afterwards, but I could tell that everybody was already forgetting everything about it— the head of the camp and the camp counselors and the other campers and the other mothers and the other fathers and my mother and my father and even that I myself was, even though I was trying with all of my might to be the one person who never would.

I felt like God was ashamed of me. I felt like God was sorry that I was the one which he had picked out and that he was getting ready to make a new choice and to choose another boy instead of me and that I had to hurry up before God did it, that I had to be quick about showing God that I could be just as amazing again as I used to be and that I could do something else.

It was August.

I was feeling the strangest feeling that I have ever felt. I was standing there with my parents and with all of the people who had come there for the field day and I was feeling the strangest feeling which I have ever felt.

I felt like lying down on the field. I felt like killing all of the people. I felt like going to sleep and staying asleep until someone came and told me that my parents were dead and that I was all grown up now and that there was a new God in heaven and that he liked me better even than the old God had.

My parents kept asking me where did I want to go now and what did I want to do. My parents kept trying to get me to tell them where I thought we should all go now and what was the next thing for us as a family to do. My parents wanted for me to be the one to make up my mind if we should all go someplace special now and what was the best thing for the family, as a family, to do. But I did not know what they meant—do, do, do?

My father took the shield away from me and held it in his hands and kept turning it over and over in his hands and kept looking at the shield and feeling the shield and saying that it was made of buckram and felt. My father kept saying did we know that it was just something which they had put together out of buckram and felt. My father kept saying that the shield was of a very nice quality of buckram and was of a very nice quality of felt but that we should make every effort not ever to get it wet because it would run all over itself.

I did not know what to do.

I could tell that my parents did not know what to do.

We just stood around and people were going away to all of the vehicles that were going to take them to places and I could tell that we did not know if it was time for us to go.

The head of the camp came over and said that he wanted to shake my hand again and shake the hands of the people who were responsible for giving the Peninsula Athletes Day Camp such an outstanding young individual and such a talented young athlete as my mother and father had.

He shook my hand again.

It made me feel dizzy and nearly asleep.

I saw my mother and my father get their hands ready. I saw my father get the shield out of the hand that he thought he was going to need for him to have his hand ready to shake the hand of the head of the camp. I saw my mother take her purse and do the same thing. But the head of the camp just kept shaking my hand, and my mother and my father just kept saying thank you to him, and then the head of the camp let go of my hand and took my father's elbow with one hand and then touched my father on the shoulder with the other hand and then said that we were certainly the very finest of people, and then—he did this, he did this!—and then he went away.

# WOULDN'T A TITLE JUST MAKE IT WORSE?

---

HOW COME IS IT I am always telling people stories and people are always construing my stories to be stories as in *stories*? Why would I want to tell people made-up stories? I can't stand made-up stories. It makes me sick to hear a made-up story. Look, if your story is a made-up story, then do me a favor and keep it to yourself. Me, I would never tell a made-up story about anything, let alone about myself. I respect myself much too much for me ever to stoop to just making something up about myself. I don't get it why anybody would want to tell a made-up story about himself. But the even bigger mystery to me is why, when you tell them the truth, people go ahead and look at you and say, "Oh, come on, quit it—noooooooooooooo." Take this one, for instance. I mean, suppose we just get us a squint at how this one works with someone like you instead of with anyone like anyone else, okay? It was when I was lecturing someplace far away from home once. I was there for the week, had to be there for the week, was signed up to teach fiction-writing there for the week—and was, for the week, being put up at the home of some very fancy folks, dignitaries in the English department or in the literature department or in one of those departments like that, both husband and wife. Anyhow, they were very grand and very nice and very kind, and I accordingly start to begin to feel so tremendously and irredeemably in debt to these folks even before I'd even slept under their roof for even one night. Well, I wasn't actually under their roof, as it were, but was in a sort of apartment affair attached to the main house by a sort of connective passageway, you might say, since passageways, I suppose, connect. I only mean to say that my place, my borrowed place, the place lent to me, that is, had its own window and its own door and when you went out of it, the door, you stepped into a little connective consideration that put you right up against the kitchen door of the grown-up house, as it also were—which is to say, the house of one's hosts. Anyhow, to get right to it if you don't mind all the hurry—you just have to appreciate the fact that I am the most fastidious little thing in all the wide and untidy world. In other words, let's say I happened to have been your house-guest for a period of ten years. Look, to give you an idea of how fastidious a little thing I am—at my usual base rate of one squillion tidinesses per year, it works out to the fact that you would find not just your house but your next-door neighbors' houses about ten squillion times tidier than they were when I had first put in an appearance in your neighborhood ten years before. So I guess it goes without saying that this little tiny sort of garage apartment I was in was the last word in presentability the

morning I was—the week's work now a job safely behind me—
making ready to leave. Okay, I had to catch a plane, you see. So
here's the deal—had positioned a box of candy on the table by
the door, had leaned up against the box of candy a square of
writing paper on which had been entered the written expression
of my gratitude, had situated the key on the table so as for the
key to act as a discouragement against the thank-you note's drift-
ing to the floor, had taken one last look about to make certain
nothing would offer the slightest invitation to reproach. Ahhhh.
Good Gordon. I tell you, I felt as if, praise God, I was getting
away with murder and was fooling them here and there and everywhere . . . one . . . more . . . time. And at this he shoulders his
carry-all and goes for the knob with his other hand. But lets go of
it, the doorknob, in the instant, it having just been disclosed to
him that he is going to have to race to the latrine, and this with
all possible speed. Now, then, we are hastening ahead in order
that we might consider the forthcoming event from the dainty
standpoint of hindsight, eh? Are you following me? Try to follow me. I have wiped. I have, as is my custom, wiped—wiping
with soap, wiping with water—and wiped and wiped and
wiped, flushing all the while. Good. I have not tarried for too
long a time. I can make it to the airport in more than enough
time. Wonderful, wonderful. I get to my feet, draw up my
trousers, fasten them, yank a handful of toilet tissue free from the
roll for to give a last finishing touch to the porcelain, to the seat,
to the whole fucking glistening commode. When I see—in the
bowl—*in the bowl*—a single, rock-hard, well-formed, fair-sized,

freshly minted stool. So I activate the flushing mechanism. The water goes into its routine commotion, the excretum gets itself sucked out of sight, but in due course—just as I had guessed, just as I had guessed—hell, *guessed*—I knew, knew, knew!—from the instant I was *born* I knew!—are you kidding, are you kidding?—it, this thing, this twist of Lishness lifts itself back into blatant view, grinning, I do believe—even, it seemed to me, winking. Fine, fine—I hit the plunger again, already knowing what there is to be known, what there is *always* to be known—namely, that I and that all my descendants might stand here at our frantic labors flushing toilets until the cows came home, that when they did come home, this malicious, hainted, evil turd would still be here for them to see, and see it—it idly, gaily, gigantically turning in the otherwise perfect waters below—they, the bovine police, would. What to do, what to do, what to do? I mean, I could *see, foresee*, feel myself beaten by *forecast* galore. This blightedness, this foulédness, it would never be gone. If I snatched it up and hid it away in my carry-all, the contents thereof would smash into it and mash it into a paste that would then smear itself remorselessly onto my favorite stuff, the best of which I had toted with me to this outpost to show myself off in in front of whosoever might show up in my class. If instead I went to the window with it and dumped it overboard, would my hosts not come and discover it (it!) beneath the very porthole the very minute my plan had seen me gone? What of taking it in hand, going to the door with it, and then going with it (oh, God, *it* again!) with me thither, thereafter to dispose of same in a suitable municipal receptacle as soon as I was well clear of the neighborhood? Yes, yes, yes, this seemed the very thing! Until foresight (*stories, stories, stories*) made me to read in my mind—in my mind—the sentence predicating the presence of my protectors there in the passageway on the other side of the door, they foregathered in beaming bonhomie for the very purpose of embracing me the one last time, thereupon to send me all the more cheerily off. So are you seeing what I in my mind—*in my mind*—saw? I would fling open the door and *he* would be there to reach for my hand to clasp it quickly to his own. Whereas were I to have taken the precaution of having shifted the turd into my *other* hand, then would that not be the hand that *she* would then shoot out her hand to to seize, *no es verdad?* I mean, I do not know what this means, *no es verdad*—but can you think of what else there is for me to say? Except, to be sure, to report to you—yes, yes, yes!—that, yes, yes, yes, I ate it. Well, of course, I ate it. After all, had it not been written that I would? Come on, quit it—has not every outcome by the teller—by me, by you, by Willie, by your aunt Tillie—already been foretold?

So now which is it, do you say—story or *story*, truth or *truth,* or words as words just working out as words?

# MR.

# GOLDBAUM

---

PICTURE FLORIDA.

Picture Miami Beach, Florida.

Picture a shitty little apartment in a big crappy building where my mother, who is a person who is old, is going to have to go ahead and start getting used to not being in the company of her husband anymore, not to mention not anymore being in that of anybody else who is her own flesh and blood anymore, the instant I and my sister can devise good enough alibis to hurry up and get the fuck out of here and go fly back up to the lives that we have been prosecuting for ourselves up in New York, this of course being before we were obliged to drop everything and get down here yesterday in time to ride along with the old woman in the limo which had been set up for her to take her to my dad's funeral.

It took her.

It took us and her.

Meaning me and my sister with her.

Then it took us right back here to where we have been sitting ever since we came back to sit ourselves down and wait for the neighbors to come call—I am checking my watch—about nine billion minutes ago.

Picture nine minutes in this room.

Or just smell it, smell the room.

Picture the smell of where they lived when it was both of them that lived, and then go ahead and picture her smelling to see if she can still smell him in it anymore.

I am going to give you the picture of how they walked— always together, never one without the other, her always the one in front, him always shuffling along behind her with his hands up on her shoulders, him always with his hands reaching out to my mother like that, with his hands up on her shoulders like that, her looking like she was walking him the way you would look if you were walking an imbecile, as if there were something wrong with the man, wrong with the way the man was—but there was nothing wrong with the way my father was—my father just liked to walk like that whenever he went walking with my mother, and my father never went walking without my mother.

I mean, that is what they did, that's how they did it when I saw them—that is what I saw when I saw my parents get old whenever I went down to Florida and had to see my old parents walk.

Try picturing more minutes.

I think I must have told you that we made it on time.

Only it was not anything like what I had been picturing when I had sat myself down on the airplane and started keeping myself busy picturing the kind of funeral I was going to be seeing when I got down to Florida for the funeral my father was going to have.

Picture this.

It was just a rabbi that they went ahead and hired.

To my mind, he was too young-looking and too good-looking. I kept thinking he probably had me beat in both departments. I kept thinking how much he was getting paid for this and would it come to more or would it come to less than my ticket down and ticket back.

I felt bigger than I had ever felt.

I did not know where the ashes were. I did not know how the burning was done. There were some things which I knew I did not know.

But I know that I still felt bigger than I had ever felt.

As for him, he took a position on one side of the room, the rabbi stood himself up on one side of the room, and me and my sister and my mother, we all went over to where we could tell we were supposed to go over on the other side of the room, some of the time sitting and some of the time standing, but I cannot tell you how it was that we ever knew which one to do.

I heard: "Father of life, father of death."

I heard the rabbi say: "Father of life, father of death."

I heard the guy who was driving the limo say, "Get your mother's feet."

Picture us back in the limo again. Picture us stopping off at a delicatessen. Picture me and my mother sitting and waiting while my sister gets out and goes in to make sure they are going to send over exactly what it was we had ordered when she called up and called our order in.

Maybe it would help for you to picture things if I told you that what my mother has on her head is a wig of plastic hair that fits down over almost all of her ears.

It smells in here.

I can smell the smell of them in here.

And of every single one of the sandwiches that just came over from the delicatessen in here.

Now picture it like this—the stuff came hours ago and so far that is all that has. I mean, the question is this—where are all of the neighbors which this death was supposed to have been ordered for?

I just suddenly realized that you might be interested in finding out what we finally decided on.

The answer is four corned beef on rye, four turkey on rye, three Jarlsberg and lettuce on whole wheat, and two low-salt tuna salad on bagel.

Now double it—because we are figuring strictly half-sandwiches apiece.

Here is some more local color.

The quiz programs are going off and the soap operas are coming on and my sister just got up and went to go lie down on my mother's bed and I can tell you that I would go and do the same if I was absolutely positive that it wouldn't be against my religion for me to do it—because who knows what it could be against for you to go lie down on your father's bed?—it could be some kind of a curse on you that for the rest of your life it would keep coming after you, until ha ha, just like him, that's it, you're dead.

My mother says to me, "So tell me, sonny, you think we got reason to be nervous about the coffee?"

My mother says to me, "So what do you think, sonny, you think I should go make some extra coffee?"

My mother says to me, "I want you to be honest with me, sweetheart, you think we are taking too big of a chance the coffee might not be more than plenty of coffee?"

My mother says to me, "So what is it that is your opinion, darling, is it your opinion that we could probably get away with it if I don't put on another pot of coffee?"

Nobody could have pictured that.

Nor have listened to no one calling and no one imploring us to hold everything, keep the coffee hot, that they are right this minute racing up elevators and down stairways and along corridors and will be any second knocking at the door because there is a new widow in the building and an old man just plotzed.

You know what?

I don't think that you are going to have to picture anything.

Except for maybe Mr. Goldbaum.

Here is Mr. Goldbaum.

Mr. Goldbaum is the man who sticks his head in at the door which we left open for the company which was on the way over.

Here is Mr. Goldbaum talking.

"You got an assortment, or is it all fish?"

That was Mr. Goldbaum.

My mother says, "That was Mr. Goldbaum."

My mother says, "The Mr. Goldbaum from the building."

Now you can picture a whole different thing, a whole different place.

This time it's the Sunday afterwards.

So picture this time this—my sister and me the Sunday afterwards. Picture the two different cars we rented to get out from the city to Long Island to the cemetery. Picture the cars parked on different sides of the administration building which we are supposed to meet at to meet up with the rabbi who has been hired to say a service over the box which I am carrying of ashes.

Picture someone carrying ashes.

Not because I am the son but because the box is made out of something too heavy.

Now here is a picture you've had practice with.

Me and my sister waiting.

Picture my sister and me standing around where the offices are of the people who run the cemetery, which is a cemetery way out on Long Island in February.

I just suddenly had another thought which I just realized. What if your father was the kind of a father who was dying and he called you to him and you were his son and he said for you to come lie down on the bed with him so that he could hold you and so that you could hold him so that you could both be like that hugging with each other like that to say goodbye before you had to actually go leave each other and you did it, you did it, you got down on the bed with your father and you got down up close to your father and you got your arms around your father and your father was hugging you and you were hugging your father and there was one of you who could not stop it, who could not help it, but who just got a hard-on?

Or both did?

Picture that.

Not that I or my father ever hugged like that.

Here comes the next rabbi.

This rabbi is not such a young-looking rabbi, is not such a good-looking rabbi, is a rabbi who just looks like a rabbi who is cold from just coming in from outside with the weather.

The rabbi says to my sister, "You are the daughter of the departed?"

The rabbi says to me, "You are the son of the departed?"

The rabbi says to the box, "These are the mortal remains of the individual which is the deceased party?"

Maybe I should get you to picture the cemetery.

Because it's the one where we are all of us getting buried in— wherever we die, even if in Florida.

I mean, our plot's here.

My family's is.

The rabbi says to us, "As we make our way to the gravesite, I trust that you will want to offer me a word or two about your father so that I might incorporate whatever ideas and thoughts you have into the service your mother called up and ordered, may God give this woman peace."

Okay, picture him and me and my sister all going back outside in February again all over again in February again and I am
the only one who cannot get his gloves back on again because of
the box, because of the canister—because of the motherfucking
urn—which is too heavy for me to handle without me holding
on to it every single instant with both of my hands.

The hole.

The hole I am going to have to help you with.

The hole they dug up for my father is not what I would ever
be able to picture in my mind if somebody came up to me and
said to me for me to do my best to picture the hole they make for
you when you go see your father's grave.

I mean, the hole was more like the hole which you would go
dig for somebody if the job they had for you to do was to cover
up a big covered dish.

Like for a casserole.

And that is not the half of it.

Because what makes it the half of it is the two cinder blocks
which I see are already down in it when I go to put down the urn
down in the hole.

And as for the other half?

That's the two workmen who come over from somewhere I
wasn't ready for anybody to come over from and who put down
two more cinder blocks on top of what I just put into the hole.

You know what I mean when I say cinder blocks?

I mean those blocks of gray cement or of gray concrete that
when they refer to them they call them cinder blocks.

Four of those.

Whereas I had always thought that what they did was fill things back in with what they took out.

Unless they had taken out cinder blocks out.

You can go ahead and relax now.

It is not necessary for you to lend yourself to any further effort to create particularities that I myself was not competent to render.

Except it would be a tremendous help for me if you would do your best to listen for the different sets of bumps the different sets of tires make when we all three of us pass over the little speed bump that makes everybody go slow before coming into and going out of the cemetery my family is in.

Three cars, six sets of tires—that's six bumps, I count six bumps and a total of twenty-six half-sandwiches—six sounds of hard cold rubber in February of 1986.

Or hear this—the rabbi's hands as he rubs the wheel to warm the wheel where he has come to have the habit of keeping his grip in place when—to steer, to steer—he puts his hands out on the wheel.

But who hears the rabbi think this?

"Jesus shat."

That's it.

I'm finished.

Except to inform you of the fact that I got back to the city not via the Queens Midtown Tunnel but via the Queensboro Bridge since with the bridge you beat the toll, that and the fact that I

went right ahead and sat myself down and started trying to picture some of the things which I just asked you to picture for me,
that and the fact that I had to fill in for myself where the holes
were sometimes too big for anybody to get a good enough picture of them, the point being to get something written, to get
anything written, and then get paid for it, get paid as much as I
could get paid for it, this to cover the cost of Delta down and
Delta back, Avis at their Sunday rate, plus extra for liability and
collision.

One last thing—which is that no one told me.

So I just took it for granted that where it was supposed to go
was down in between them.

# SQUEAK IN
# THE SYCAMORE

---

I WANT TO TELL YOU some fast things first about when I was
little and then I am going to go ahead and tell you a story like
everybody else. One is there was a tree out front and I heard things
in it and I could not see up to the top of it and it made me scared I
couldn't. Two is the man next door said come see my jonquils and
I did not know if I should or not. Three is I went to bed with socks
on and somebody came in and pulled off the covers and stood
looking and crying and saying look at that. Four is Little Eugene
had a slime spoon and they made it my job to be the one to have to
go clean it off. Five is the butter-and-egg man died from adhe-
sions. Six is the plumber died from getting electrocuted. Six is the
gardener died from digging up a basilisk. Seven is the electrician
died from a double hernia. Seven is the fruit-and-vegetable man
died from his goiter getting wet. Eight is my second-grade teacher
died from something. Nine is the sandwich man at the druggist's
died from something else. Ten is the mailman died from kidney
trouble and his wife. Eleven is the man who came to put the wallpaper up died from keeling over. Twelve is my mother died from

stones in her cunt. Thirteen is my cousin Artie Sakowitz died from choking on ice water. Fourteen is Aunt Esther died, Aunt Dora died, Aunt Adele died, Aunt Pauline died, Aunt Miriam died, also Uncle Lou did, Uncle Sig did, Uncle Jack did, Tante Ida did, Tante Lily did, and so did a girl in my class from bending over too much, and so did a man from a sled hitting his head, and so did a dog, and so did Jesus. Lots of movie stars are dead. Rabbi Sandrow is dead. There are dead people from wars, from volcanoes, from floods, from earthquakes, from fires, from famine, from pestilence, from pestilence, bad food, bad habits, rash decisions, rushes to judgment, killer plants, death thoughts, from playing too much with a jump rope too much, from even just doing nothing. There is a bug that can make you die by you walking on its back. There is a jellyfish that can swim in through your nose and then climb up into your brain and then eat your whole brain up. There is a lake that has bloodsuckers in it that can suck all of the blood out of somebody and nobody can get the bloodsuckers off of them even after all of the blood has been sucked out of them and there is no blood left in them anymore for the bloodsuckers anymore to suck out of them anymore. Did you know you can get somebody's hair stuck in your throat and suffocate from it? You can get hemorrhages. You can get dysplasia. You can get glossitis and herpetic stomatitis. You can get acute arterial thrombosis. Don't laugh. It's not funny. There's nothing funny about any of it. You think there's anything funny about obstructive uropathy? How about idiopathic long QT syndrome, you asshole! You think it's funny too? Fucking people with their fucking idea of what's hilarious! It makes me sick when somebody's got pericarditis with effusion and people start laughing about it and making wisecracks about it and carrying on like it's some kind of fucking joke.

People!

What makes people so absolutely so sickening?

Doesn't anybody know what makes people so sickening?

Okay, as to the story like everybody else:

Schmulevitz comes out of the doctor's office, and Mrs. Schmulevitz says to him, "So? So what is the verdict?"

"The verdict?" Schmulevitz says. He says, "You are asking me, Schmulevitz, what the verdict is? Because the answer is," he says, "not so hotsy-totsy, for your information. Because, for your information, Mrs. Schmulevitz," Schmulevitz says to Mrs. Schmulevitz, "because for your information the man gives me two weeks tops."

"Two weeks tops?" Mrs. Schmulevitz says to Schmulevitz. She says to him, "You are telling me the verdict is two weeks tops? So what is the deal with the two weeks tops?" Mrs. Schmulevitz says to Schmulevitz. "What, pray tell, is the condition with regard to the two weeks tops?" says Mrs. Schmulevitz.

"The ticker," says Schmulevitz. "The man says to me forget it, Schmulevitz, it's the ticker. Tops, the man says to me, you got two weeks, tops, the man says to me, period. This is what the man says to me because of the ticker," says Schmulevitz.

"Well," says Mrs. Schmulevitz, "at least thank God it's not cancer."

So to you that's pretty fucking comic, right?

God, I cannot goddamn believe it.

# THE DEAD

---

DEAR, DEAREST PEARL,

Just a note to say how sorry I am that I cannot be with you to visit with you before you turn two days old. The trouble is I'm sort of snowed in up here in a northerly city and they're saying there won't be any way out of it for me for a while. It makes me feel just awful to have to be kept away from you like this. Your mother and dad called on up here last night to pass along to me the news about you being in the world with us and all. I'm glad. I'm so glad. It's just terrible the way the weather way up here is keeping me away from you. I never saw such weather—snow, snow, snow—and the wind blowing it past my window with such meanness. How is it wind can get like this, so wild and nasty and mean? I'm not only way up here in this northerly city, but I'm way up high in this hotel. Maybe the wind wouldn't be so bad if my room was on a lower floor—or maybe it just wouldn't seem to me to be so bad—everything, the wind, the cold. I mean, maybe the wind would seem to blow by slower or something. I don't know. I'm just miserable about the whole thing, me stuck here like this up here like this, and you down there getting ready to be a day older without me there to sit in there with you on the passing of the time. It's probably warm where you are—indoors, inside, all that sort of thing. I'm indoors too, inside too, but it feels pretty terrible to me in this room. God, Pearl, it's so white outside—but you know what? When I get up close to the window, I can see there's a skating rink down outside there out across a kind of park kind of deal just opposite from here over on this side of the hotel. Can you believe it, people skating when it's weather like this? There's a lot of them out there, it looks to me like, going around and going around. It looks easy the way they're doing it, but I bet you it's hard—what with so much wind and so much cold. Imagine it, your feet freezing in your skates and the wind getting you better than ever every time you make your turns. But none of them, those skaters, are showing off anything but the greatest of ease to me from way up here. Of course, I'm way up. It's such a high floor I'm on and the hotel couldn't be a bigger one if it tried. What made them ever want to make such a big hotel way up here so north? But I suppose nobody way up here can really tell what it's really like way down there. Maybe it's not so bad. Maybe I'm just making it sound bad because I do not know what else to say. I guess they're probably having fun, all of them, the skaters. They're going around. I can hardly see them the way you can hardly see people from here. But they're skating, all right. It's the white. It's the snow flying, whiting everything out—or whiting it way down anyhow—making everything seem so faraway-seeming. It is like a dream. Did you know my mother's dead? Did you know my father's dead? Did you know my sister's dead? Pearl, I know you're not even two days old yet and I know it's probably not the best thing for me to be sitting here talking to you about dead people yet, but I just wanted for you to hear it first from me—my mother's dead, my father's dead, my sister's dead—and lots of other people, they are dead too. There are so many dead other people. They died of different things. I had the idea I should tell you. If I get another idea I think you should know something about, I'll let you know, okay? But this is it for the time being. Plus saying hello to you and welcome to you, and I love you. Just this one other thing, Pearl. I really like the name your mother and dad gave you. I mean, it's got a lot in it for a name, I think. It goes, I think, with all these things I'm seeing in the world today—and thinking of today and missing so bad, so bad, so bad today. Pearl, Pearl—I am just saying your name. I hope you're warm. I hope everybody's warm. If you ever go skating, be careful—oh, please. Get something bright and put it on. How about you put on a red scarf or something? Or it could be a red cap. Then maybe people won't bump into you maybe—and maybe somebody will be certain to be able to see you and to keep seeing you and to never stop seeing you—even from a long way off. Oh, and another thing—keep going, Pearl—don't stop going, don't ever stop going—because otherwise what will happen is they will come and come and bump you from behind the back.

Your grandfather,
Gordon

# IMAGINATION

———

X WAS A TEACHER of story-writing, and Y was a student of same. X was a remarkable teacher of story-writing. In the opinion of A to Z, exclusive of Y, X was the best teacher of it there ever was. Still, Y sought out X for instruction—for although Y was not willing to hold X's skills in the very highest esteem, Y nevertheless held them in esteem high enough. Perhaps he viewed X's great gifts as a teacher as meriting X the status of second-best, whereas the first-best had nothing to teach Y.

Y was a hairy person, and very grave in his manner. X, on the other hand, tended toward the bald, and was lighthearted in all save two respects—his wife being one and stories the other. In these two matters, X kept up his purchase on the world as he thought it was, never cracking a smile in relation to either topic, a practice that Y thought foolish and tiresome. But of course Y had neither wife nor a vocation for living inside stories. Y wanted to write them, create them—and, as for women, he amused himself with reptiles instead.

Listen to X commenting on Y's stories, the which he judged the weakest among those produced by the class.

"What's this dragon doing in here? Why a dragon?"

"Dinosaurs are extinct. Write about the world as it exists in our time."

"Very good, except for the snake. The snake's a *deus ex machina*. Don't you see? You can't just stick a snake in here to resolve the conflict people have produced."

X shouted. X was passionate about stories. In X's opinion, that's where reality got its ideas from. Y, for his part, listened with interest. After all, Y had sought X out to learn.

"For God's sake, man, why pterodactyls? Can't you make it a family of farmers instead?"

Y would smile. He had such a lot of hair and it all seemed to smile right along with him when he did. It made X think of Samson, all this ferocious growth, and of his own near-hairless surfaces. Poor X, his body was weak, but his mind, he observed, was very strong.

Then X met Z.

Oh, Z!

Z was neither teacher nor student of the writing of stories. Z cared not in the least for stories, and surely would take no position in the debate between X and Y. Z's enthusiasms were restricted to the parts of her body and to the uses that might be made of them.

How can it be that such a creature would come to fall within the ken of X?

In one version, Y proposes her, presenting her to X as Y's

barber, the person whose attentions account for the vigor of Y's hair.

In a second version, X's wife is the agency through which X and Z meet, the former woman having heard that the latter can do wonders in the contest against thinning hair—restore growth, prolong vitality, work a miracle.

In either version, Z did—barbering X before and after his classes, a program Z kept up until Z's husband came back to her, thus making it necessary for X and Z to find another privacy for Z's talents to continue going forward in the matter of X's hair.

Insufficiency of it, that is.

Here's where Y comes into it again.

In one version, X and Y are quarreling about one of Y's stories, and X decides to give ground in order that he might then beg of Y a certain favor—in vulgarest terms, the use of Y's bed.

In a second version, Y remarks on the improved condition of X's hair, whereupon X, for whom everything is a story except stories that are not real, sees the way to make this one "come out," resolving the conflict that people have brought about, this without resort to some damned *deus ex machina*.

In either version, X and Z get Y's bed.

Or were about to, that is.

For it would first be necessary for Y to give X a set of keys and a caution, which latter was this—to vacate the premises before a certain hour, there being a cleaning woman and a delivery person scheduled to put in appearances at Y's at that hour in the first case and shortly thereafter in the second.

Did X understand?

He did.

It was not difficult for the teacher to be instructed by the student since, apart from the writing of stories, X appreciated he had everything to learn. On the other hand, this wasn't much— since, for X, very little stood apart from the writing of stories, the major exceptions being X's wife and now, of course, Z. And besides, Z only counted in what she did for X's hair.

In X's opinion, both before and after this story, he wouldn't have had any of it if it hadn't been for Z.

Now, in a good story, the reader would be entitled to know why. What was it that lay at the root of X's unlucky hair? Didn't X have a lady without a letter to massage his scalp, finger it with enriched shampoos?

He did.

In one version, this very question occurs to X himself—and in the same version, he is unable to answer.

In a second version, the wife is absorbed by her interests as much as X is by his, typing being the only one that really seems to persist in her.

True enough, it was a means of supplementing the meager income produced from X's teaching. And anyway, didn't she also type for X—his lecture notes, his comments to students, though never a story he'd made up?

X did not have to make up stories. Those that were written for him to read and hand back were, in his opinion, quite enough.

"Be out by two sharp," Y warned. "Because the cleaning lady comes right when I told you on the dot."

"Good God," said X, unimaginative as usual, "you certainly don't expect me to let her in."

Y sighed in weariness with expectation coinciding with event.

"Of course not. She has her own keys," Y said.

"Two o'clock?" said X, wishing to make certain he was not uninstructed as to fact.

"Um," Y said. "She promised to be there in time to let the delivery in."

Now to the good parts.

Z was undressed.

Naked.

Not a stitch on her barber's body.

And she had carried it all into the bathroom to urinate and to place into position her device.

X, for his part, sat on the bed, his hair-deprived being quivering with desire—too, it must be admitted, with spasms of anxiety set astir by what X now sees showing in the space between the floor and a certain closed door. Through the crack a red light glows—a red light in a closet? Shining? Even an ordinary light would be something to wonder about—and X's brain went to work, invoking its powers to proliferate fictions, imagine revisions, get scared.

A hidden camera? Maybe even a sound-recording mechanism, too. Yes, of course! It's a setup. Y, Y, Y! It's revenge for all the criticisms, for "Very good, except for the silly snake."

X betook himself and leapt off the bed.

"Stay where you are!" X called to Z. "Don't be alarmed," he counseled manfully, "but I think there's something up," and with this X crossed the tiny apartment to fling open the worrisome door.

X would have screamed had there been any breath in him to do it. He threw his shoulder against the door and shoved as strenuously as a man with too little hair could. But the thing had its nose against the bottom of the door. When it came to pushing it back in, X was no match for what was pushing its way out.

It lumbered sluggishly toward the center of the floor as X flew back to the bed, jumped up on the mattress, and threw himself against the wall.

That's how the cleaning lady found them—Z locked in the bathroom and X trembling against the asylum of the wall. It was she who got the thing back into the closet, where its feed was and where its bowl of water was and where the infrared bulb did its best to simulate the temp of its natural habitat. She just shooed it back in there with a broom, more startled of course by naked, glabrous X and the small shrieks borne from the bathroom than by the giant lizard that slumbered heavily in the middle of the apartment floor.

"It's called a monitor lizard," Y told X years later at a cocktail party celebrating the publication of Y's first collection of stories. "Dead now—couldn't take the climate. African, you know. Largest of the land lizards."

"I thought the Komodo was the biggest," said X, trying to put the best face on things.

"Well, you know," Y said, and turned to greet another ardent admirer, leaving X to doubt even the little he dared to claim.

That story ends here. But this one goes on for a bit.

In this story, the end has different versions.

In one version, the delivery was a manuscript, and the person making the delivery was Y's typist—who is, of course, X's wife, and who arrives in time to see the cleaning woman gathering up the clothes anticipated by the man who is standing on the bed.

In another version, we have Y inscribing a copy of his book for presentation to his old teacher, X.

He writes: *Things always work out for the best. With affection and appreciation, your grateful student, Y.*

And then there is the name of the city—and the date.

# RESURRECTION

---

THE BIG THING about this is deciding what it's all about. I mean, by way of theme, what, what? Sure, it gives you the event that got me sworn off whiskey forever. But does that make it a tale of how a certain person got himself a good scare, put aside drunkenness, took up sobriety in high hopes of a permanent shift? I don't think so. Me, I keep feeling it's going to be more about Jews and Christians than about this thing of matching another man glass for glass. But I could be wrong in both connections. Maybe what this story is really getting at is something I'd be afraid to know it is.

Either way or whatever, it happened last Easter, which doesn't mean a thing to me because of me being Jewish. To my wife it's something, though, and I am more or less willing to play along—providing things don't get too much out of hand. Egg hunts for the kids, this is okay, and maybe a chocolate bunny wrapped in colored tinfoil. But I draw the line when it comes to a whole done-up basket. I don't see why that's called for, strands of candy-store grass getting stuck between floorboards and you can't get the stuff up even with a Eureka.

As for the Easter that I am talking about, not much of all of this was ever at issue. This was because we got invited out to somebody's place. I think the question just got answered this way—whatever they do, that'll be it, that'll be Easter—no reason for us to have to make any decisions. Which was a relief, of course—the whys and wherefores of which I am sure you do not need for me to explicate for you. But my wife and I, we found something else to get into a fuss about, anyway. And that's the best I can do—say "something else." Because I don't remember what. Not that it was anything trifling. I'm certain it must have been something pretty substantial. I mean, aside from the whole routine thing of Easter.

But our boy got us reasonably jolly just in time for our arrival. What happened was, you just caught it from him, his thrill at getting into all this country-ness. You see, I think our boy really suffers in the city—I think my wife and I agree on this—not that you could ever actually get a confession of his unhappiness out of him. He's all stoic, this kid of ours—God knows from what sources. Twelve years old and tough as a stump, though to my mind that is still nowhere near as tough as what I think you have to be. At any rate, he was out and gone as soon as we pulled up into the driveway. Trees, I guess. That boy, in him we're looking at a mighty delight to get up high on anything, his mother and his dad always hollering, "Come down from there! You're giving us heart trouble!"

The host and hostess, they were swell people. No need to say more. Nice folks. I was going to say "for Christians," but it is never necessary to actually say it, is it? As for the house-guest thing, we can skip right from Friday when we got there to Saturday before supper, them having over a few neighbors to meet us, other couples, more Christians. There was this one fellow among them, he seemed to take me for a person of special interest. We got to talking with what was surely more gusto than the rest. I don't know what about so much as I know it had to do with a lot of different municipal things—the houses around there, the gardening, getting the old estates up to scratch with strenuous renovations. There were these trays of Rob Roys going from hand to hand, and dishes of tiny asparagus spears and something lemony in a small porcelain bowl, kids underfoot, and the light in there was that country light, this burnished thing the April light can sometimes get to be at maybe any o'clock when you are indoors in a low-slung, high-gloss, many-windowed room. Well, I might as well tell you now, the fellow had a little girl there, maybe half the age of our boy. Harelipped—this was the thing—a girl with a bad face to go through life with, and I think I got drunk enough to say to the man, "Aw, God—aw, shit."

That's it. The story stops short right then and there where I was. Because the next thing I know, it's morning and I am waking up in one of the upstairs beds. But I cannot tell you how I got there. I cannot even tell you what was what between when I was having those Rob Roys and just standing there and when I was lying down and pulling away the comforter from my head.

There was a carillon across the street. Or across the town. Who knows? It was playing hymns. Or what I think are hymns.

As for me, I felt entirely terrific—feeling nothing, not even a tremor, of what you would expect in the way of aftermath. I mean, I had gotten so bad off that I had actually lost time, lost hours of real life. But there I was, waking up and never sprightlier, never more refurbished in fiber and spirit. Restored, I tell you—I could have said to you, "Look at me, for Christ's sake, look at me—I am in the pink!" Except for this thing of a whole night having vanished on me—that was something I wasn't going to think about yet—or didn't really actually even believe yet—whereas I kept trying to figure out how a thing like this sort of worked, one minute you're on your feet blazing away with a great new friend, the next minute you've skipped over no knowing what, and how did you get to here and to this from that and whatever that *was*.

Thing was, I knew I couldn't ask my wife. Christ, are you kidding? But I could smell the bacon down there, and went down, thinking that if I don't get a certain kind of a look, then this will mean I must have behaved passably enough, even if I was actually out like a light behind my eyes. And that's how the whole thing down there turned out, all of them downstairs— host, hostess, wife, our boys—and nobody—wife least of all— seeming to regard me as other than an immoderately late-riser and indecorous latecomer to the holiday table.

Coffee is poured, conversation reinstalled.

But here is where the story stops short again. Because—just by way of making an effort to add myself to the civilities—I said, "Wretchedest luck, that guy, and such a handsome woman, his espoused, the two of them such a damnably attractive couple, and that little girl with the, you know, the thing, the lip." I mean, I did a speech as an offering, as a show of my harmless presence, the hearty closing up of the morning circle, the one we seek to form to ward off what there was of night spells.

Not stops short enough, though. Because somebody was taking me up on it, converting ceremony to sermon. My wife, of course—her, of course—with that carillon going wild behind her. I tell you, whoever it was, and whatever he was playing, the man was good on the thing, the man was getting something colossal from those community bells.

But back to my wife, please—for she nips off a bit of toast and says, "You call that bad luck? Knowing what you know, how could you call that just a piece of bad luck, just a harelip?"

Ah, but this is madness, this is hateful—saying anything about a thing like this when I know it is a thing that ought to be left unsaid. Besides, we had no business being where we were. Even if it had meant keeping to the city and to squabbling over everything in sight, here is where we belong, where we never should have strayed from, where all the trees worth climbing are in a reasonable park. Those were rich people. My drink, when I was drinking, it had never been anything too mixed.

I mean, what the hell was she getting at, just a harelip?

I didn't give her the satisfaction. I didn't ask. What I did was go to work on it with my own good sense—trying harder to remember, or to make things up—the result being that on the way home, I came up with a thing that goes roughly like this—the fellow with the little girl sort of producing himself from out of the midst of the rest, me not tracking his features any too clearly, my vision already diminished by at least half.

"Ah, yes," he says, and with his glass he gives my glass a click. He says, "Great to meet the neighbors, don't you say?" He says, "See the fucking neighbors?" He says, "Here's to fucking us."

And me, what did I do? Say *l'chaim*? Click his glass back?

"Oh, sure, sure," I hear him say. "Sure, sure—right, right—fine, fine—swell."

I know. We drank.

Did I ever say, "Surgery can handle that"? Is that what I said? Or "It's nothing—they've got ways to fix that right up"?

I mean, what had I said to him to get him to say to me, "Had a little chap of his measure once," and lift his Rob Roy in salute to my boy? Except that I am just guessing that he was doing that—because by then it was too hard for me to see if the man was really pointing anybody out. "Bloody garage door took his fucking head off, don't you know? No, really, old chap. Brand new electric sort of a thing. Electronic, I mean.

We were coming up on a toll-booth, my wife and I. In real life, that is. But I don't have to tell you that I wasn't there with all my wits. "Take this!" my wife was saying, and I took a hand off the wheel to take the coins from her hand, meanwhile still making up sentences to keep filling in for whiskey.

"Nothing against the old homestead, though—no fucking hard feelings."

Is that what I think the man said next? Or something like, "The fucker drops like a shot the day they finish getting the wiring in."

I don't think I ever got his name, the man who came for cocktails when the neighbors came over and who then left so that the hostess could finally sit us down to something—my wife says cold lamb. She also says she was standing right there and heard every single word, him saying how they'd lost a son but that God had made it up to them with the girl. My wife says the man said to me, "I'd spotted you, you know," and that I said, "For what?" and that the man then said, "For a Jew."

But maybe my wife was making that up, too, just the way that I am making this up, especially the part about me hearing the son of a bitch say, "Happy fucking Easter," and me seeing myself get a hand up out of my pocket to hold his chin in place so that I could aim for right on his lips when this was where I kissed him.

So for what it's worth, that's the whole story, and notice, won't you, who just told it cold-sober.

# SPELL

# BEREAVEMENT

---

MY SISTER SAYS, "It's Daddy. It's about Daddy."

My mother gets on and says, "Don't cry. He will be all right. Please God in heaven, God is taking him into his loving embrace right this minute and the man will be all right."

My sister gets back on and says, "Daddy just went a little while ago. Daddy is gone."

My mother gets on and says, "I can't talk. Don't make me talk."

My sister gets back on and says, "So make up your mind, are you coming or not?"

My mother gets on and says, "No one could begin to tell you. You turn around and the man is gone."

My sister gets on and says, "We have to have your answer. So which is it, are you coming or not?"

My mother gets on and says, "Like that." My mother says, "Just like that." My mother says, "You couldn't believe it." My mother says, "I couldn't believe it." My mother says, "You blink an eye and that's that." My mother says, "Did you hear me, were you listening to me?" My mother says, "You blink an eye and it's goodbye and good luck."

My sister gets back on and says, "Now is when you have to decide. Not next year, not tomorrow, not after we hang up. Do you understand what I am saying to you? I am saying now, make up your mind right this minute now while we are sitting here talking to you because we do not have all day for you to wait around and for you to decide."

My mother says, "There wasn't an instant when I didn't expect it, not for years was there a single instant when I didn't expect it. But you think it still didn't come to me as a surprise? I want you to know something—it came to me as a surprise. I can't breathe, that's how much it came to me as a surprise."

My sister gets on and says, "Do you realize we have to make plans? So what are we supposed to do if we don't know how to plan because we don't know if we're supposed to plan for you to come down or not?" My sister says, "Be reasonable for once in your life and tell me do we plan for you to come or do we go ahead and not make plans?"

My mother says, "My head never once touched the pillow when I didn't expect to wake up with the unmentionable staring me right in the face." My mother says, "I want you to hear me say something—all of my life with that man I had to sleep with one eye open." My mother says, "Did you hear me say that? Did you hear what I said?" My mother says, "Please God that God is listening, because I as the man's wife never got a moment's rest."

My sister says, "Make up your mind. Are you making up

your mind? Here, speak to Mother, tell Mother. Mother wants to know if your mind is made up."

My mother gets back on and says, "Talk to your sister, I can't talk."

My sister says, "So is it yes or is it no?"

My mother says, "The man was my husband. For going on sixty years next month, the man was my husband. So were you listening to what I said to you, almost sixty years next month?"

My sister says, "Is it the fare? You need us to help you with the fare?"

My mother says, "You don't have the money to come to your own father when the man is dead?"

My sister gets on and says, "We have to make arrangements. We have to make calls."

My mother says, "Do you know what it costs to call from Miami to New York? Do you want for me to tell you what it costs for somebody to call from Miami to New York? Do you think they give you free calls when somebody is dead and you are calling from Miami to New York?"

My sister gets on and says, "Look, no one is saying that this isn't just as much of a blow to you as it is to us. But we can't just sit here and wait all day for you tell us what, if anything, you are going to decide to do. So once and for all, yes or no, you are coming or not?"

My mother gets back on and says, "Let me make one tiny little suggestion very clear to you—where there is a will, there is a way."

My sister says, "Let bygones be bygones—just say yes or just say no and whichever it is you feel you have to say, we give you our absolute assurance that we will do our very best to completely understand."

My mother says, "Talk to your sister. Try to make sense."

My sister says, "Don't tell me. Tell your mother. Your mother has a right to hear you express yourself as honestly as you can."

My mother says, "Take this, take this—I don't want to touch it—I can't even breathe yet, let alone pick up a telephone and talk."

My sister says, "You're making her sick. I already gave her a pill and now you are making your mother sick." My sister says, "I'm telling you, the woman has taken all she can take." My sister says, "If I could afford it, you know what?" My sister says, "If I had the wherewithal to do it, if I had the money lying around to do it, you know what?" My sister says, "I would run get a doctor for her even if I had to beg, borrow, and steal to do it for her because the woman should be given a good once-over by a good doctor, hopefully a specialist who is absolutely topnotch." My sister says, "But thank God the woman doesn't need it." My sister says, "Thank God the woman has the strength of a horse."

My mother says, "All his life the man was not a big money-maker. But you know something? The man was good."

My sister says, "Let's be sensible. Let's bury the hatchet and work things out together. Do we plan for you to come down or do we not plan for you to come down? Give me a simple yes or no and we will know how to conduct our affairs after we have to hang up."

My mother says, "I am here to tell you, the man never made a fortune, but you cannot say the man was not too good for his own good."

My sister says, "I don't know how the woman is still standing on her feet. Don't torment her with this. Don't you know that you are tormenting her with this? Stop tormenting your mother."

My mother says, "The man was too good. But do they give you a medal for being too good? Listen to what I am telling you, your father was too good. The man was goodness itself. You know what your father was? Your father was too good for this world, this is what your father was."

My sister says, "I want you to know that I am getting ready to wash my hands of this." My sister says, "Are you waiting for me to hang up?" My sister says, "Is that what you are waiting for, are you just sitting there waiting for us to hang up? Because if you want for me to get off, believe me, I can get off."

My mother gets back on and says, "The man was a saint." She says, "Listen to what I said to you, did you hear what I said to you?" She says, "Ask anyone—a living saint."

My sister gets back on and says, "No one is saying this is easy for you. Do you think it is easy for me? But things do not get done without plans being made, and things have to get done within no time at all without fail." My sister says, "I have to make certain calls. People have to be called. I am trying to call people and get things taken care of without causing Mother any undue excitement or any additional upset." My sister says, "Consider your mother's health. The woman is not young. The woman is totally devoid of any reserves of energy to draw from should, God forbid, worst come to worst. So don't make worst come to worst. Try to appreciate the fact that the woman is at her wit's end. The woman has not one more shred of energy left over for anymore of your crap. So do I make myself clear? Or do I have to spell this out for you what I am saying to you when I say eighty-eight? Do I have to tell you what your mother has already been through today and she only just an hour ago woke up? So are we going to get your answer or are we going to have to scream ourselves hoarse? Because all your mother wants to know is if she and I are supposed to expect you to come down here or if we are not. So are we or aren't we? Or is it your instruction to us that we are to go ahead and plan your own father's memorial service without his beloved son? Is that what your instructions are?"

My mother says, "You don't have to do me any favors. You do not have to do anybody any favors. Do as you please. If you want to come, come—if you don't want to come, don't come—the world will go on very nicely with or without you. Your father does not require your presence if it is too big a bother for you to come to the man when he really needs for you to be here in attendance here."

My sister gets back on and says, "Is he listening to us?"

My mother says, "It is not a necessity. There is no necessity. If you can't make it, you can't make it. Not everybody in the world can always be expected to just drop everything and run. I promise you, it is no disrespect if you couldn't make it. No one would accuse you of nothing. Your father would not accuse you of nothing. Your father would be the first person to tell you to do what you have to do if it is a question of prior business making a prior claim on you which couldn't be avoided at any cost. If it's business, don't give it a second thought. So which is it, business or not business? Because if it is business, then it's all well and good. Believe me, your father would be the first one to go along with the fact that not everybody has a situation where they can afford just at the drop of a hat to take time off from their business, come rain or come shine."

My sister says, "If it's the money, then maybe Mother can get you something out of savings and reimburse you when you get down here for whatever you had to lay out for it out of your own pocket. So talk to Mother, tell her what your situation is, tell her what you have in mind, make a clean breast of it with her and get it out on the table with her and I am sure a solution can be found and it will all work out. But if all it is is the ticket down and the ticket back, you could see who maybe has a special on right now for night flights if you left tonight sometime. So why don't you maybe call up around town and get the best price and then call us right back?"

My mother gets back on and says, "The man only wanted the best for his family." My mother says, "The man's every waking thought was for no one but his family." My mother says, "The man could never do enough for his family." My mother says, "The man never wanted one thing for anyone but his family."

My mother says, "His family's happiness, this alone is what gave the man life." My mother says, "Wait a minute—not his family's happiness, but your happiness—yours, you, the professor, the poet, his darling, his son."

My sister says, "This has gone on long enough. I am not asking again. Yes or no? Either answer the question or forget about it, because I am hanging up."

My mother says, "It is no crime if you cannot come. No one is going to say that there should be a finger pointed at you if you cannot come. You come or you do not come, you only have to suit yourself."

My sister gets back on and says, "Don't kid yourself, it is a crime, it is a sin, it makes me sick to be his sister."

My mother gets back on and says, "I am just trying to think what would make the most sense for all parties concerned."

My sister gets back on and says, "Drop dead. He should do everybody a favor and drop dead. Did you hear what I just said to you? He makes me sick."

My mother gets back on and says, "Be nice. Don't fight."

My sister says, "I am giving you one more chance." My sister says, "Do you want another chance?" My sister says, "As God is my witness, this is your last chance."

My mother says, "He's listening, he's listening." My mother says, "Don't worry, he's listening." My mother says, "Talk turkey to him, tell him what the situation is."

My sister says, "Your mother wants to hear your voice. Try to act like a human being. Let the woman hear your voice."

My mother says, "Talk to me, darling. I am listening, darling. Let me hear my darling talk."

My sister says, "Let him go ahead and drop dead. Stop begging him. Stop babying him. Stop pampering him. You know what would serve him right? If he hung up the phone and dropped dead."

My mother says to me, "Your father loved you like life itself." My mother says to me, "You know what your mother is saying to you when she says to you like life itself?"

My mother says to me, "Speak to me, sweetheart."

My mother says to me, "Talk to me, sweetheart."

My mother says to me, "Tell your mother what it is which is in her darling's heart of hearts."

What is in my heart of hearts?

There are not people in my heart of hearts.

There are just sentences in my heart of hearts.

So what was I to say to them?

Not to the locutions of discourse but to my mother and my sister.

Because I really honestly do not think that there was any way for me to say to them why I was not answering what they said. I mean, let's not be ridiculous. You can't just turn around and say to people—good God, not to your own most beloved loved ones—that you are too disabled to talk, given that what you are doing is meanwhile going crazy with pencil and paper so as not to miss scribbling down every single word.

# THE DOG

---

I WAS NEVER in a place like that. I was an American boy when they had places like that. So everything I say is just me imagining things. Except for the names, of course. I know the names. I have a list. I have been making a list. You couldn't guess the names I already have on it. But I am not anywhere near finished yet. There is just no telling what it is going to take for me to get the list completed. Because the point of this is that they only want you to hear about a handful. They only want you to hear about the same ones which they want you to hear about, which are the same ones everybody all over the world has already heard about. Whereas there were secret ones. There were hundreds of them. Even hundreds is a big understatement. They had them everywhere. You couldn't guess where they had secret ones. You would faint dead-away if I told you where they had some of them. You would think what a liar I was if I told you, or was crazy or was worse.

Here is one of the famous ones that is known to absolutely everybody.

Ravensbrück.

You probably heard of that one.

I think it sounds like a name.

Not like Oswiecim.

Imagine having to say Oswiecim morning, noon, and night. That is probably why they called it Auschwitz, even though Auschwitz wasn't its real name.

But take my real name.

I should put my real name on my list.

What if they had a barber at Treblinka, at Buchenwald, at Dachau? I have been thinking about this. What if they had to have a barber to get all of the hair off of them for when the women came and the girls came—get off all of their hair everywhere—didn't they do that, take off their hair off for something, didn't they take it all off of the girls and off of the women for some us-hating purpose?

So they must have had a person who did it. They must have had a person who cut the hair off. It must have been a person who would be good at it and who would not get tired from doing it and who would know how to keep doing it, just cutting and cutting and not giving the wrong answers. Because look at how hard it would be just to keep doing it, you would have to be a one-hundred-percent professional—all of those girls coming in at you and taking their clothes off and all of those women coming in at you and taking their clothes off, and your job is to keep on cutting their hair off without letting them think that you are doing it for any other reason other than the one that it is all for their own good—to help them keep clean, to help them keep their health up, to save them all of the bother of washing it and of combing.

So what do you think about the question of who did it?

You think they would give the job to what kind of a person?

Tell me which gender, at least, and how old in years you would want this barber of theirs to be.


Between 1938 and 1944, I made regular visits in from Long Island to my father's place of business. It wasn't just my father's business. It was his business in business with his brothers. It was the business of making hats for women and then of getting Macy's and Gimbel's to buy them in big quantities just to begin with. My father would show me around to all of his workers and then call up for his barber to come up to give me a haircut, and then a man came up and did it.

Then this is what my father would say.

"Now that you've been cleaned up, let's go out and put on the dog."

Then my father would give the man the money and take me out to a Longchamps for lunch and then, later on, to DePinna's for something new, like new leggings.

The money my father gave the barber, here is how he did it.

He slipped it to him.

You know, slipped it—a way you work the hand.


Birkenau.

Carthage.

Oz.

New York.

# FISH STORY

A S FAR AS I was always concerned, the outdoors was where
you maybe went when it wasn't raining and only when
you had to. I wasn't the only indoorsy type in my parish to cher-
ish this unhealthy opinion. One thing was, you couldn't hear *Jack
Armstrong* under some spreading chestnut tree—because Jewish
boys did not have spreading chestnut trees and, anyway, back in
those backward days, portable radios went about three pounds
shy of the total tonnage of the *Normandie*, crew and cargo loaded.
Or maybe they hadn't even invented them yet—portable radios,
I mean, not Jewish boys. But the days were indeed backward, all
right, aglow with the feeble light those ancient flame-shaped
amber bulbs struggled to give off. Everybody's mother thought
they were the cat's pajamas, those cunning bulbs, just the thing
for the fake-Tudor houses everybody lived in. Oh, we were all as
happy as clams in those glowy places the mothers tried to pry us
from into the bright outdoorsy day calling all unwholesome
boys. All you wanted weekdays was a box of Uneeda Biscuits or
a row of Walnettos, to sustain you from *Jack Armstrong* through
*Lorenzo Jones*. Saturdays, *Let's Pretend* and *Grand Central Station* so

filled the inner kid and stilled the organs of ingestion, you went serenely, the whole day, without. Sundays we won't even talk about, so that you will not have to hear what it sounds like when a grown man sobs. Oh, I suppose I can risk a little bit, mention just *The Adventures of Nick Carter, Master Detective*, and *Quick as a Flash*, and then leave it, I think, impressively at that.

Are you kidding me—the outdoors? The outdoors was for droolers and for nose-pickers, for kids called Buster and Butch and for the one, I swear, called Bix. The outdoors was for the kid we called "Wedge" because, you know, because someone had told us your wedge was your simplest tool.

But sometimes God was merciless and it did not rain.

It was then that the mothers came armed with reminders of Green Harvey, to storm the trenches of Bad Hygiene.

But first they'd move into action with rickets.

*You'll get rickets!*

(Aw, Ma, what's rickets?)

*Rickets is from not playing outdoors and from eating meat from a can! Do I ever give you meat from a can?*

(Aw, Ma, I've got to stay tuned for a coded message.)

*Tell me something. Mr. Young-Man-Who-Is-Willing-To-Break-A-Mother's-Blood-Vessel, have you lately taken a good look at Harvey Joel Rosensweig?*

Visions of Green Harvey a menacing number of houses down always did the ruthless trick. Because you did not want to look like Harvey Joel Rosensweig anymore than Harvey Joel Rosensweig did. And if you were the sort of chicken-hearted impressionable that I was, the mother in question did not have to break a blood vessel. You want to divide a believer from the family Emerson, you will never get a better crowbar than Visions of Green Harvey. But this, of course, was back when liddlies were just little.

And that was another thing they hadn't invented yet—smart kids. Not only that, but they also hadn't *un*invented parents who never heard of traumatizing the crap out of a ten-year-old idiot.

Green Harvey!

Jeepers, you never saw a kid quicker when it came to buckling on his swashes.

So there you were, on the lawn, just crazy to participate in the American Way of Life. You had the Wheaties box to guide you in the modalities of how your American boy is supposed to play, but what you didn't have was anybody to do it with—because this was the day it was your mother who was the only mother home to hound her issue into the streets, all of the other mothers being at the neighborhood rummy game, where it is that the mothers and fathers in a perfect world were always meant to be.

I'd sit on the curb for a time and stare at some glinty thing in the gutter. I don't know what it was with me, but in those backward days, whenever I sat on a curb, this is what I would do, cut my eyes sideways from side to side until I had spotted some glittery thing, a bonanza in the gutter. Then I'd sit there, at whatever distance, trying to guess what it was. Not guess, really, but just declare aloud with mad conviction—because the point was that you were always something magical, Renfrew of the Royal Mounties or Sergeant Preston of the Yukon, alone like this, the startling powers in you something scary in your solitude, and you of course would just simply *know* whatever it was, off there in the gutter—not even needing a second glint.

Gum wrapper!

And then I'd get up and go look.

The time's too backward for me to remember if I ever guessed right. But I remember one day what it was when I'd guessed wrong, and it is this that accounts for my getting into this whole outdoorsy business with you in the first place.

Because one day it was a fishhook.

Now a fishhook in the gutter was not a discovery you routinely made in the gutters of the streets where I come from. I'm talking about a place called the Five Towns, a sort of way-station along the ongoing Diaspora about twenty miles out on Long Island, counting from the center of familial concern—which was the New York City where all of the fathers bravely went each day with their brown suits and their hats of gray.

I wasn't all that dumb about fishing, mind you. Not only did I know it was a thing the Wheaties box okayed, but I knew that almost all the grammar-school readers had Skippy always doing it with his dad, or Bucky always wanting to do it with his pa, or Franklin Delano Roosevelt letting him see you do it with his dog.

I knew they all did it with an animal they called a worm and with a stick they called a pole.

I knew they got *worm* and *line* and *pole*, and that where they then went with them to to a *crick*.

I wasn't too sure we had anything around there where we lived that would qualify as a crick, but the first three items I figured for a cinch. Hook in hand—you know, *holding* it—my mother's shrieked philosophy conjuring the shout of calamity in my ear (*You will put an eye out with that thing!*), I headed for the garage, happy to be in darkness for the time it took to get the pole (a piece of picket fence, an upright left over because the lawn we had did not go that far) and the line (a bunch of Venetian-blind cord the vermin had set up for themselves as a haven in a heartless world).

Worm.

Worm?

I'd seen a few in my time—but not really where they had come from. I mean, a worm was something Green Harvey would come running at you with—until you had seen him coming and took off a safe distance the other way, far enough for his fat to make him quit coming and eat it—the worm. But it never crossed my mind to wonder where Harvey Joel Rosensweig got his worm from. I suppose I just leaped to the conclusion you had to be a Green Harvey to get one.

Worm! Worm! Worm!

I think I remember scuffing up the pebbles in our driveway for a trice or two, giving many maddening seconds to my idea of how a real American boy breasts all hardship for him to quest the Great Quest. What I mean is that I was by this time back in those backward days pretty damn wised-up as to a pessimist's construction of everything in sight—meaning: if I did not catch a fish, I would be the last one to be surprised I didn't. Listen, it was a boyhood perpendicular to the kind you read about in the readers in school. It was a boyhood where the community prepared for disaster and was amazed when it did not strike. It was a boyhood where standards were sky-high but where expectation had been leeched out of them to make a safely null class. Hey, I'm not whining—I am just giving you the whole heart-rending picture.

So here we are, nostalgia fans, back behind the family garage with a piece of picket fence, about nine feet of chewed-up Venetian-blind cord, and a hook Satan had set out to do temptation's work there in a gutter-looker's gutter.

It took about a half hour to walk it to the crick, an inlet (let out by the Atlantic Ocean) spanned by a little bridge you crossed to get to the beach clubs. We called that inlet The Inlet, and we called the bridge The Bridge—not unmindful of how Skippy and Bucky were always coming up with these really great names for things—it dawning on me that if you got yourself out there on a little poke of dock up on out there on the landward side (hello, Skippy! hello, Bucky!), you could drop a line down into something liquid deep enough.

Look, I can appreciate how knot-tying is probably a pretty big deal to most people, but for me there's never been much in it after the shoelace stage. So if you are wondering how I got that

Venetian-blind cord stuck onto that piece of picket fence, save your worry for the hook. Because the hook, jeez, it truly was a bitch. I mean, I tried a lot of very fancy thinking, but my brain could only handle the thought that it definitely could not be done unless you had a derrick. So I just dropped my line in, tossed my Venetian-blind cord in, hookless but serious-looking if you went by the principle of its having lifted up and lowered back down again lots of put-upon slats.

So how else could this all come out but as a good and counter-vailing lesson for a boy who always waited for the worst?

I am not saying that what happened converted an indoors type to an outdoors one. I still get closest to God somewhere where you can control the light. But I will just say that I went ahead and pulled up no fewer than a dozen lunatic fish with that stick of picket fence—fish that just bit anywhere *all at once* on that Venetian-blind cord and would not let go of it wherever they'd bit on a bet.

I did not take even one of them home to prove it, though. As a matter of fact, I did not even take one of them off the line. I just dropped that stick of fence and ran like hell, all twelve or so of those infectious things still on there fastened to it, their killer jaws clamped there in a kid-killing smirk.

Oh, I can see how it is probably true that Green Harvey might have stuck around—the loon might even have harvested those evil-hearted monstrosities, to pitch one through the window of every mother's son who had ever believed himself to be far enough away from undoing indoors. But I had had my fair warning at what is sometimes under outdoor things, and I knew that I did not want to know what really fishily was.

It was better than thirty years later, when I was turning the pages of a Ladybird Book for an indoors type of my own (a kid whose peaceable opinion of nature continues to treacherously thrive on an abundance of urban ignorance), that I found out what it was that the Wheaties box had got me into back when my heart was still brave and true—namely, the worst scare ever to chase me through all of the backwardness of my youth.

It was just a blowfish.

They were just blowfish—every last one of them all blown-up certitude in himself.

He'll bite on any fool thing, your natural blowfish will. But so, for that matter, will your friendly reader—hook, line, and sinker. I mean, since it is all the same in the end, and if it is all the same to you, give me human nature every time—and the equally calamitous fishing of men.

# GUILT

———————

I FELT ADORED. I felt adored by people and things. Not loved
merely. Adored, even worshipped. I was an angel, born an
angel. I recall knowing I did not have to do anything particularly
angelic to be viewed in this light. I was blessed, or I felt blessed. I
don't think this feeling came into being exactly. I don't think it
grew as I grew. I think it was with me right from the start. It was
what I stood on. It was the one thing I was sure of. It moved
with me when I moved. It was acknowledged by everything that
saw me coming. Animals knew it, the dogs in the neighborhood
knew it, all the parents knew it, not just mine. The sidewalks
knew it. If I picked up a stick and held it, I knew the stick was
holding me back, would be willing to embrace me if it could.
Everything held me back or wanted to. The sky wanted to reach
down with its arms when I went out to play.

I had blue eyes and blond hair and I was very pretty. I was
favored in these ways, it is true. But I was not vulnerable on account of it. I mean, the condition of adoration in which I understood myself to be held was in no respect contingent upon prettiness. This was not an opinion of mine, not anything susceptible

to test, proof, refutation by argument or circumstance. To say this understanding was conditional would have asserted nothing more than the testimony that experience is conditional.

Of course.

Let's not be silly.

I wish I could think of a way to get speech into this without disrupting things. But I don't think I can. If presences could talk, I could do it. Presences are what counts in what I'm getting onto paper now that I am forty-seven. The people don't count. Not even Alan Silver counts. Besides, I cannot remember one thing Alan Silver ever said. Or what anybody else did.

Here's what I remember.

I remember blessedness until I was seven. I was safe.

Then we moved to a different neighborhood, another town. The war was on, and I think my father was making money off it. He had more money, however he got it. This was a certainty, no speculation. In the old neighborhood, we were renters. There was some vague shame in this, being renters. I knew about it. The boys I played with must have said so, or their nannies must have. I supposed they were trying to interfere with the magic that encircled me. I supposed they envied me. Envy had been explained to me. I don't know who did it. I suppose my mother did. I suppose she taught me, told me to expect envy, to be ready for it, not to be surprised by it, to fortify myself, stay vigilant.

I admit it, it didn't work. There was shame attached to renting even if it was envy that inspired them to let me know that's what we were, that's what we had been, renters in a neighborhood where everyone else owned.

Moving did not defeat this, though. What I mean is, between the time I knew we were going to move and the time we moved, I didn't fight back. I didn't tell the nannies we were going to own. I don't know why I didn't. I think I must have thought moving was more shameful than renting was, even if you were going to own.

Perhaps I thought we have to go someplace else to own, that we can't own here.

I don't know.

It wasn't that terrible.

That's how safe I was, how adored I felt myself to be, even by the nannies. Especially by the nannies.

I'm telling everything.

The nannies adored me because I didn't have one. This was a bonus. It was reverence on top of what I already had from them. The shame of renting was the same. It supplemented the universal blessedness. It was shame and it was intended that I be shamed by the knowledge, but it also abetted the well-being I was supposed to have. The nannies and the boys they took care of understood that my interests were secured, perhaps heightened, to the extent that humiliation was heaped upon me.

I understood this.

I understood it was queerly superior to be less well-off.

I understood it was a good thing for me to be a child like this, but not a good thing for the grown-ups whose fault this was.

The shame was really theirs. I shared in it only insofar as I could profit from it, be esteemed as more angelic because of it.

But then we moved.

The old neighborhood was old in relation to houses. The new neighborhood was new in the same way.

Houses were still going up.

You have to imagine this—a plot of land, everything dug up, mud mostly, three finished houses, five finished houses, seven finished, but everything still looking unfinished.

It stayed this way for years. Even after the war was over, it still looked like this, unfinished.

They all had money from the war. This was what people said. People said it was war profits that got us these new houses. The maids said it.

There were no nannies in this neighborhood.

The maids were black and they didn't like the people they worked for. When it was only children around, the maids talked so that the children would hear them. In the afternoons, before they started getting the suppers ready, the maids stood out on the street near enough to where the children were playing. Profiteering was a word you heard because it came up a lot—*them*.

There was mud all over everything every season of the year. In the old neighborhood, everything was finished and had a gabled roof or long dark beams crisscrossing over creamy stucco, turrets on the corners sometimes. And there was grass.

I'm telling you about the profiteering part only to show you how charmed I was. Let's see if you understand.

Listen. Let's say I was seven and a half, eight, not yet nine. But I knew. I knew war profits was much worse than renting. I knew the maids hoped to put a malignancy abroad, hurt the children who heard it, make sure we heard them saying *them*.

I heard it. It didn't harm what held me higher than the rest.

Alan Silver did that. It was Alan Silver that brought me down.

Here's what happened.

Alan Silver moved in. He moved in when there were seven houses and four more still going up. He was twelve. Maybe I was nine by then. So that's the boys from two houses. The other five had boys in them too. There were girls, of course. All the houses had girls, but I can't remember any of them. Except Alan Silver's sister. Oh, there's only one reason I remember her. Or one memory she is in.

The girls didn't count.

I can't tell you how much the boys did.

I was the youngest. Then came Alan Silver. The rest were older. But I don't know how old. There were five of them, and they were rough. Maybe they weren't rough, but I thought they were. This opinion derived directly from their policy respecting the mud. I mean, they played in it, or they picked it up and packed it and threw it at people. If they threw it at me, I sat down until it dried up. If they threw it at one another, they kept on playing.

They never threw it at Alan Silver that I ever saw. But I never saw Alan Silver play outside. I don't know where he played. Maybe he played inside. Maybe he went to another neighborhood. I never played with Alan Silver. I never talked to him. I never looked at him up close.

But I saw him. Everybody saw him. Everybody talked about him. Not the boys or the maids but the parents. The parents said he was an angel. He looked like an angel. He had blond hair and blue eyes and was pretty the way they said I used to be—but he still was, even though he was twelve.

It was when I came across this belief that I felt changed. I hadn't been noticing what was happening. I had been outgrowing my prettiness and I hadn't noticed. Isn't this amazing? To stop being the most beautiful?

For the first time ever, I felt unsafe. For the first time ever, I felt they could get me, it could all come in at me and get me, penetrate, kill me, find me in my bed, choke me and my parents wouldn't try to stop it, would sooner have Alan Silver instead.

I'll tell you how I handled this. I stopped going outside so much. I stayed away from where I might get mud thrown on me—and if it happened that I did, then I didn't wait around for it to dry first but went home right away to wash it off. This meant making worse tracks inside the house. So it didn't handle anything any better, because the maid yelled or my mother yelled or they both yelled—and when they did it, I could see them yearning for Alan Silver in my place.

I could see desire.

The way I used to feel the sky would put down its arms for me if only it had them, I could see a heart red in the sky just above the roofs—a red, red heart.

It was desire. It was the desire of a neighborhood. It was everything, all earthliness, God too, desiring Alan Silver instead.

The first thing I heard was the siren. I was in the back of my house staying clean. Maybe the maid heard the siren first. Maybe she ran to the front door first, or maybe I did. But what I remember is the both of us at the door looking out.

The fire engine is up the block. By the time we are there looking out, the firemen aren't in it. Then there's screaming. But the maid and I stand in the door.

The screaming's from over there, over on this side, and from this side comes Alan Silver's mother and Alan Silver's sister, and they're the ones screaming, and I never heard screaming like this before, all this screaming all the way from over on this side to all the way up the block, and Alan Silver's mother is pulling at her hair, or maybe she is pulling at the sister's hair as they go running up there to where the fire engine is parked. Then everybody is running out of all the finished houses. They are all screaming and going to where the fire engine is, but keeping a little behind Alan Silver's mother and behind Alan Silver's sister even if they started out from a closer house.

I don't know what thing amazes me more—people pulling at their hair, or the fire engine on the block, or seeing the whole neighborhood outside all at once.

The whole neighborhood is out there where the fire engine is and where the firemen are coming out of an unfinished house, the very last one at the end of the block. Then they go back and then they come out and then they go back and then they come out, and it's then I notice the maid's not standing with me where I am standing anymore.

My house is empty except for me.

They all went up there where I knew something terrible was.


I went in.

I went back to the room where I'd been. I think it was the kitchen or the breakfast room. I went back to eating my milk and cookies again.

In the whole neighborhood, I was the only one who didn't go up there. But wasn't I too young to see a thing like that?

I knew it had to be a thing like that.

Days later, they started talking about it—the parents, the maids, but not any of the kids.

I could tell in the doorway—or I could tell when I was eating the milk and cookies I went back for.

He lived in a coma for a while. But I knew he would be dead.

They said the five boys were playing with him when he fell. They said he fell from where the top floor was going in. They said he fell down through the shaft where the chimney was set to go in—to the concrete they had already poured down in the basement for the basement.

I remember thinking, "What was Alan Silver doing playing with those boys?" I remember thinking, "Was he always playing with those boys when I was staying clean?"

"Someone pushed him," I thought.

"I thought, "Which boy did?"

I wanted to tell everyone I didn't.

I am forty-seven years old.

I still want to say I am innocent.

# SHIT

---

I LIKE TALKING about people sitting on toilets. It shows up in the bulk of my speech. Wherever at all in keeping with things, I try to work it in. You just have to look back at stories I have had printed to see that I am telling the truth. People on toilets is certain to show up with more than passing incidence. I will even go so far as to say that where you find a story with a person on a toilet in it, forget the name that's signed as author—no one but me could have written the thing. Indeed, it is inconceivable to me that I didn't.

But the one I've got now, this one here, it promises to be the best of the bunch.

Or anyhow the purest.

Well, the truest, then—the one with nothing in it made up.

The other thing about it that I like is that it could not be simpler to tell—nothing in it but just a man sitting on a toilet in it and the wallpaper in it that the man is looking at.

Oh, of course—not just a man but myself, in fact—the one who is doing all of this telling right here this very instant.

How would I tell a story about anyone else? For one thing, it could never be true, could it? I mean, what do I know about anyone else—or care to? Good Christ, I have all I can do to marshal even a small enough interest in myself.

Or do I mean large enough?

I don't know.


That's another thing I am always putting into stories—"I don't know." Just those words, just like that. You see a story with "I don't know" in it, that'll be the tip-off to you as to who definitely was it who wrote it. It could have anybody down there under the title there—but he isn't.

It's exciting. It is exciting.

Not writing, not speaking—but being a sneak.

When I was a boy, that was what I wanted to grow up to be—a person who was an assassin and a sneak. I wanted to be dangerous. That was when I was little.

When I was little, my mother would get me to sit on the toilet and stay there and stay there until I could show her something, and sometimes—more and more often—I couldn't. She would say, "Put your royal bombosity down on the royal throne and don't you dare let me see you get up off of it until there is something in there in it for me to look at."

It's terrible what I have to show for it now. I tell you, I don't know where the food goes. It's frightening. Am I getting poisoned from way up inside?

I take things. You know—to make me go.

I especially take things when we go away and it gets worse—

not going, the not-going. That's where this comes in—the story, this story, the wallpaper. Listen to this—I'd taken a lot of something—because it had been days already, days of nothing but of sitting and of not going already, maybe even a week of it. So I'd swallowed enough to choke a horse, gone to bed, been down for mere minutes, when I had to get back up again and I really mean it, *get back up!*

It was somewhere quaint—an inn somewhere—you lose track—a cute hotel—meaning no bathroom of your own, meaning a bathroom out at the end of the hall, meaning a bathroom with a kind of a latch contraption on the door—and a pitched ceiling pitched so low you had to keep bent over—even sitting down, I had to stay bent down—and even bent, I couldn't stop going—oh, God, just going and going—forever it felt like, gallons it felt like—it felt like my whole life was coming up—or out.

I mean out.

Which is when I started studying the wallpaper.

I thought I was sluicing away into death, dissolving from the inside out, rendering myself as waste, breaking down to basal substance, falling through the plumbing, perishing on a toilet I could not even call my own.

You'll laugh, but I got scared.

I thought: "Call for help."

I thought: "Do it before you swoon."

Which is when I reached out for the wallpaper as you would for a lifeline, for smelling salts, a float.

I don't know.

I thought: "Hang on to the wallpaper."

I mean, with my mind, with that.

Well, I could see it was a wallpaper you could do it with—a pattern—growing things—things that grow—a picture of this, then of that—and the names for them thus:

Blue-eyed grass.

Wintergreen.

Sweet William.

Sneezeweed.

Vetch.

Violet.

Primula.

Coreopsis.

Clover.

Mariposa.

Marsh marigold.

Rose mallow.

Dandelion.

Red-eye.

Clover.

Black-eyed Susan.

Poppy.

Bluebells.

Hepatica.

Buttercup.

Wood sorrell.

Belladonna.

Ivy.


I swear it—all those, each and every one.

Grasses, weeds—I don't know—crap, all that itchy, actual crap, pointless from the word go.

I sat there holding on.

I mean to tell you this—that I had had the thought that I was doing it for nothing less than life. Pretty dumb, right? After all, all it was was just a lot of shit. If anything, I should have been joyous, been jubilant, been pleased as punch. Hey, come on—I was going, wasn't I?

But I was shaking like a leaf.

I thought: "Hey, hotshot, you think you're so smart, then make something out of this!"

Skip it, what the facts are—I don't trade in truth. I say you just heard a lie. I say time, it just stopped itself in its tracks.

# WHAT IS LEFT
# TO LINK US

---

I WANT TO TELL YOU about the undoing of a man. He's not a fellow I ever knew very well. It is only the key erosions that built to his collapse that I know well enough, the handful of episodes that toppled this fellow from the little height he thought he had. I, in fact, was present at what you might call the critical moment. I mean the turning when our man was tipped, as it were, all the way over. As for the math after, how he has since fared in the grip of his ruin, that is a matter I know, and care, next to nothing about.

He had a marriage, children, and a second woman whom he would see from time to time. As far as I could tell, his relations in all these respects were perfectly correct, the usual make-do life of a fellow residing in urban circumstance, a fellow in his forties, a moderately accomplished chap, which statement is meant to convey the impression of a fellow exceptionally able—if you will allow the assertion that passing accomplishment in our parlous times often calls for surpassing ability. His was that sort of urban circumstance—the work he did and where he did it. But this is just a particle of what I mean.

I won't trouble the initial sentences of this account with a description of the wife—for she will make her appearance later, when that critical moment of ours arrives, and this will do nicely enough for her, given all that she really matters to what is herein unfolding. Nor is it profitable that you know much about the second woman—and indeed I do not have that much to tell you, considering that I have laid eyes on the creature only once—just as I only once saw the woman that is the wife. It was at what I keep calling the critical moment that both women were first revealed to me, a coincidence you must have guessed was coming.

As for the children, they are positively of no consequence at all.

What I did know, and knew well before the worst happened, was this: The man who is the subject of this little history had elected to end his relation with the second woman and had gone ahead and done something toward this end. At least this is what he said he had done when he later sought my attention over cocktails.

"To which she said what?" I said, trying to concentrate on particularities that interested me no more than the larger chronicle did.

But the fellow was waiting for this. He played with his glass and let a histrionic silence draw the curtains aside. Then, suffering the phrases of his speech as if to place before me a parallel of the desolation he chose to believe the second woman had struggled to surmount, our man said:

"'If that is what you want. If that is what you must have. All right, then have it you shall.'"

"Splendid!" I said, and then I said, "You're well out of it, lad!" adding this latter more for reasons of ceremony and rhythm than in response to anything known. Surely, I had nothing substantive to go on, no basis to judge the health of the fellow's spirit one way or the other, with or without his having the second woman to visit from time to time.

But it proved he was waiting for this also.

"I don't know," he said, pretending thought, it seemed to me.

"Of course you do!" I said. "Well out of it, I say!"

"I'd like to think so," he said, fingering his glass again, not swallowing much except in showily halting motions to his mouth. "But I don't know."

"Ah, well," I said, already fashioning up the sentence that would sponsor my exit.

You see, like the fellow whose dishevelment I record, I too reside in urban circumstance. I had planned to do the household grocery shopping after hours that Friday night—to do as I have always done in order that I not have to do the household grocery shopping the Saturday morning following, the number of shoppers being half as many Friday nights.

It was, and is, my custom—and I have come to be convinced that it is only the unbending observance of custom that sustains life in an urban circumstance. Those city persons strict and exact in their habits, and in possession of a hearty dispensation of them, make it through to their Mondays. I believe I have seen examples persuasive enough on either side of the question to propose the postulate.

Such a postulate guides my conduct, in any case—whatever the validity of its content—and I had been too long drinking with this man and had good reason to be on my way.

Moreover, there was nothing I wanted to hear from him. There would be no surprises in anything he would say—he, as I, knew exactly what to say.

It is why I am not very interested in people—nor all that much in myself. We all of us know exactly what to say, and say it—the man who sat with me making an opera out of his glass; I, speaking to him then and speaking to you now; you, reading and making your mind up about this page.

There is no escape from this.

Nor is it any longer necessary to act as if there might be.

It was only necessary to say: "Look, my friend, there will be another one after this one. Better to have made an end to the thing and to get a new thing on the march."

He raised his eyes from his fraudulent musing, noticing me for the first time, I could tell.

"That's a shockingly childish suggestion," he said.

"You think so?" I said. "Perhaps my mind was elsewhere. What did I say?" I said.

He studied my expression for a time. I could see what he was after. But I would not let him have it.

"I'll get the check," he said, glancing at his wristwatch, and then, in a stylishly sweeping motion, lifting the same hand to signal for the waiter. "Got to run," he said, polishing off his drink and finishing with me as well. Then he said, "Dinner's early and I haven't done the groceries yet."

During the course of the events I describe, my son's sled was stolen. Actually, it was removed from the premises by the custodian who services the little apartment building we live in. It was our custom to keep the sled right outside the door, propped against the hallway wall and ready for action—whereas it was the custodian's custom to complain that such storage of the sled interfered with his access to the carpet when he came once a week to clean it.

He comes Saturdays.

I could hear him out there with his industrial-caliber vacuum cleaner some Saturdays ago. The rumpus the thing creates is unmistakable, and I remember having to raise my voice to repeat "Your move." It was midday, a perfectly lovely piece of weather, but we were home playing checkers, my boy and I, while his chicken pox healed and while his mother was out running errands. It was only when she returned that the theft was discovered, the place where the Flexible Flyer had stood leaning now an insultingly vacant patch of very clean carpet.

She called the landlord and she called the police.

The sled is, after all, irreplaceable, one of the last Flexible Flyers made of wood, a practice some while ago discontinued. We had to search the city to find it and buy it—and it was very satisfying to display it when the snow came and all those less demanding parents showed up with their deprived children and plastic.

I know he took it. I did not see him do it—but I know, I know.

It was a test of something, a clash of habits, custom pitted against custom—our resolve to show off our quality, his resolve to perform unstipulated work.

On the other hand, it is our carpet that is now uniformly clean those last few inches all the way to the wall. Not his!

I am not unwilling to be pleased by this.


At any rate, the man I am made to call my friend—because it is clumsy to keep referring to him otherwise, and I suppose I must say I know him as well as I know anybody—telephoned me at my office the Monday following. Have I told you that we are in the same line of work?

The fellow often calls me at my office, to speak of business. It is the basis of our knowing each other—business.

"Why did you say that?" my friend said.

"Say what?" I said.

"You know," he said. "Suggesting that I get another setup."

"Haven't you always? I thought that was your practice," I said.

"That's not the point," my friend said.

"Then what *is* the point?" I said.

"Skip it," my friend said, and hung up.

I was not the least bothered by any of this. To begin with, the man tired me—and conducted a private life no more notable than my own. It is not that I am too fine to hear a man's secrets; it is only that no one has any new ones. Besides, insofar as our joint concerns of a business nature go, the man's need of me was greater than mine of him. At all events, there is no question of it now. You must remember, the fellow has since been reduced, brought down. When it comes to need now, he is the one who has it all.

It was at the toy store everyone around here uses that I saw the fellow next. There was nothing exceptional in our meeting there. We both have children; it is the best-stocked store midtown. One is always meeting someone one knows there.

"I'm worried," my friend said. "Please give me your attention. Do I have it?"

"You have it," I said, and stared impressively at the two children whose hands he held.

"That's all right," he said.

"Yes," I said, "but it is not all right with me," at this using my eyes to usher his down to where they would notice the boy whose hand I held.

"Oh," my friend said. "Well, I'll call you."

He called that Monday.

"What's wrong with your kid?" he said.

"I thought you had something to tell me," I said.

"I do," he said, "but I never saw your kid before, and I was just thinking maybe my pal's got his sorrows too."

"Just chicken pox," I said, with my free hand squaring the papers on my desk.

"Takes a while for the scabs to heal, you know. Been through the shit twice with my two, and it can be a bitch, all right."

"Yes," I said.

"You're listening?" he said.

"Absolutely," I said, settling back now for whatever would come.

"I told you I was worried," he said. "Now here's why I'm worried."

No, no, I would never give him what he wanted. "Because you broke it off with her," I said. "And now you're worried that perhaps she's angry—and if she is angry, then maybe she will do something, make trouble—correct?"

"That's it," he said. "That's it exactly. So what do I do?"

"Do something to make her happy," I said. "Then she won't be angry."

"But what?" he said. "What could make her happy when she's angry?"

"Something special," I said. "Something uncommonly giving is what I usually recommend."

"You're right," he said, said he hoped my boy's face would soon be without blemish, thanked me for the counsel, and hung up.

The landlord claimed he was blameless, that he was not responsible for the loss of articles I chose to store outside my door, that if I dared deduct the cost of the sled from my next check in payment of the rent, eviction would ensue. I remarked that the custodian was in the landlord's employ and that logic insisted the employer be held liable for thefts perpetrated by someone acting in performance of his employer's requirements. The landlord said that logic insisted nothing of the kind, that it was not his habit to retain the services of thieves, that his employee was not a thief, and that, moreover, I had no proof of anything of the kind.

The police said their hands were tied and that the loss, after all, was just a sled. But don't think I did not take down the oaf's badge number, the one who had said just a sled.

As for the custodian, he has taken to coming on a weekday.

I am not at home weekdays.

My wife is. And she is afraid, I tell you, afraid.

My friend called. I was about to leave, and perhaps I was not paying very close attention. Perhaps I should have examined his proposal more carefully. But it was a Wednesday, and Wednesdays I always vacate my office a quarter hour sooner than is otherwise my habit, this to provide time to pick up the laundry before presenting myself at home.

I was courteous enough, I think. I do not think I was especially abrupt. But I expect I was not listening very closely. As a result, I not only failed to hear him well enough to advise him with prudence, but of course I can also have no confidence that I will reproduce his sentences accurately. I believe, however, he said something approximate to this:

"I have the thing, just the thing. A really incredibly good idea, something extraordinary and giving, just as you said. You see, the thing was she was always complaining that I was unreasonably hesitant to let her share in my world, to be with the people I was with, that sort of thing. You know the sort of thing I'm talking about—they do it all the time. I mean, once you're really involved with them, what they invariably want from you is to get really involved with you—hear about your friends, hear about your job, hear about your wife, all the dreariness that *you* of course *don't*. It gets that way with them, this pushing at you and pushing at you for more and more of your life. Oh, God, you must have had your own experiences with what I am talking about. Honestly, I really don't think they can help themselves. I mean, they *know* better, don't they? I mean, they've got to know that if they keep it up, they're going to end up pushing you too far. But they do it and they do it—and you go and do precisely what they don't want, hold back, hold more and more back, until it's yourself you figure you won't hand over anymore. The point is, that's exactly why my idea is right on the money. Because the idea I had is to give a party, a sort of going-away party—something that will give her what she wants but end it at the same time. Just me and her and my two closest pals—you and this other pal I have—because I was always telling her about the two of you guys and she was always so terribly interested. It drove me nuts the way she was always asking to meet you two, me always having to invent excuses why she couldn't, these two great buddies I have who happen to be my two best buddies, you and this other buddy of mine."

I think I remember saying, "Please, be sensible, you and I are not precisely on such terms." Or I may have said, "Please, be sensible, that is a vulgar and lunatic plan."

I do not know what I said. I know that that night, when I had emptied out my briefcase to sort my papers, I found a notation giving this man's name, a restaurant, a date, a time. I still had this in my hand, amazed, when I went to ball up the laundry wrappings to stuff them in the trash. I don't know why I did not discard the slip of paper along with the rest. You will understand that it was not because I must have said yes to the fellow and was unprepared to go back on my word. Perhaps it was because I *had* said yes and was unprepared to dishonor the queer impetus in me that had made me do it. In any event, I put the reminder in my pocket and the laundry wrappings in the trash basket, lifted out the plastic liner, cinched it, and tossed the whole arrangement down the stairwell for the custodian to find it when he would.

The bastard.

There is chicken pox and then there is chicken pox—and my boy had the second kind. We cautioned him not to scratch. Please understand that he is the quality of boy who respects a caution. I know he tried his best to resist. But a mad itching is a vile thing, and when it is rampantly in its mania, there is nothing left for it but to claw.

He did his best.

I tell my wife the lesions that left scars on his cheeks will prove a trifling matter in the years of his growth.

But she cries. She cries—when it would appear to her I am asleep.

Of course, it occurs to me to wonder if the scars are why she cries. It could be the loss of the sled that makes her cry. Or the specter of the ungovernable custodian. What kind of creature would take away what belongs to a child?

Or it could be something else she cries about.

He must have grown anxious, after all, this fool of ours—because I arrived second, and hear him say he had been sitting and waiting for almost an hour. Yet I was punctual, as is my custom. It was more than clear that he had been drinking for however long he had in fact waited. One would guess that he had come to regret what he had impulsively contrived, and it is to this that I attribute his hurried and avid indulgence.

"Are you afraid?" I said.

He tried to smile in rebuke of this, but what his ambition produced was instead a lopsided impression of grossly disordered zeal. "What kind of thing is that to say?" he said, and threw his face toward the glass of whiskey that he had been elevating a degree or so off-plumb with his lips.

"Lad, you will never make it through the evening," I said.

"Will too," he said, not in the least equipped to rearrange the distortion that had seized his features. "Never felt more alive. Never more magnificently aware. You won't be sorry, buddy boy, I promise you."

I was going to ask my friend to give me a bit of information about the man whom was still to come. Not that I really cared, but only to make conversation until the other diners arrived and the catastrophe got productively under way. It was then, while I was preparing to offer my inquiries and while my friend was laboring to raise his hand to call for a round, that I was strangely overcome by the oddest realization.

*I had never seen the custodian.*

The man might actually be anyone. The man could come running right up at me from anywhere—and I would never know that he was the man I should be ready for.

Had my wife seen the fellow?

Of course she must have—for had she not heard his complaint about the sled?

I know it will appear curious when I tell you that the matter of the custodian, my disquiet over my never having seen him, so captured my attention that I've only the scantiest recollection of the drinking and the eating and the table-talk that followed. I know that the second man proved a rather amiable chap and that we more or less discovered mutual interests. The woman was quite pleasant, really—handsome enough and not unintelligent. I cannot, I'm afraid I must say, recall much that anyone said, although I believe that the chitchat went agreeably forward and that the woman seemed genuinely pleased to be meeting the other fellow and myself. Yet she made no great effort, as I remember, to draw either of us out—nor did she appear particularly bent upon an exchange with my friend. To sum it up, she was acceptably polite and sociable, if a stroke remote, and I for one intended to respect whatever distance she seemed to wish established.

I believe I kept to that mark.

I cannot say she showed the least surprise that our fellow was becoming progressively intoxicated by great bounding leaps, or tumbles. I certainly was not—and, speaking for the other fellow, I am sure he wasn't, either. All in all, the evening was going off not a little gracefully, considering the ground we were hazarding—it all resolving itself in food and drink, a few peppery but convivial bickerings, and even some moments of downright comradely laughter.

All this time, as I have told you, it was the custodian that remained chiefly in my consideration. Or, to put the point more descriptively, it was in my mind to get him out of it—and to focus my alertness on what was enacting itself before me. But I cannot say to what extent I was able to rid my thoughts of the swinish janitor and to open them to the decorous drama that was playing at the table. What I do remember quite sharply was when my friend began nipping at my sleeve.

"Bathroom," he said.

"You want to go to the bathroom?" I said.

"Bathroom," he said, still pinching my sleeve and tugging at it.

"Lad, lad, you can manage for yourself," I said, more amused than bothered, really.

We all watched him stagger off.

He seemed to make his way well enough—stepping uncertainly, but a sure bet to carry out his mission without assistance.

We watched him go around a corner and then we fell to chatting again. I believe I introduced the matter of the sled, an unspeakable felony, an outrage that would give me no peace. I must add that my companions seemed eager enough to discuss the matter, to register as yet another insupportable instance of the trying circumstance we urban dwellers are asked to tolerate.

"Vandals," I said. "A city of vandals."

"We live in fear of plunder," the other fellow said.

And the woman added, "No one is safe."

We were getting on rather briskly with the subject, I must say. But conversation suddenly ceased when, as one, we understood our victim had been absent overlong.

Should someone go look?

The woman said, "Oh, it always takes him forever."

I recall thinking this her first coarse remark of the evening, and was a shade disappointed that this item of tastelessness was likely as far as she would let herself go. The other chap was on the point of rising when we all saw our fellow appear from around the corner, stumbling in our direction, but making reasonably effective headway.

When he had seated himself, the woman addressed him with a certain firmness. "It always takes you forever," she said, saying this clinically and not with the familiarity, on the one hand, nor with the irritability, on the other, that you might have expected, given the history that underlay our little assembly.

I believe I was astonished at how even-tempered the whole peculiar affair was turning out to be. In a way, the equable character of the evening was the least tedious aspect of it, one's assumption being that the expectable would in due course happen. Yes, I had liked it for that, or didn't. I can't think now which.

I have not asked her why she cries. Perhaps she does not know. And what is one to say of this, of knowing?

Besides, whichever of the plausible explanations she chose to give me, am I not already well versed in the plausible?

What the lesions left on my boy's face is exactly what I guessed they would. He picked at them—he could not keep himself from picking at them.

The landlord has sent a letter reviewing the procedure for the discarding of trash. He asks that I return to my customary respect for the premises. I will reply that my respect for the premises has not wavered. I will reply that I am unwavering in every respect.

I will reply that my boy will be unwavering in his time, and that my wife does not waver, either.

I wonder if it would alarm the bastard to know this.

I wonder what the bastard thinks.

I do not know how much longer we were talking and eating and drinking when our host broke his silence to say:

"Didn't take me forever."

We stared at him.

"Are you answering something I said?" the woman said.

Our host stared back, either past speech or not talking—it was not worth bothering to tell which.

"Are you responding to something one of us said?" I said.

"Telephoning," he said.

"You were telephoning?" the other fellow said. "Or is it that you want to use the telephone now?"

"Telephoning," our friend said.

"You were telephoning," the woman said, "and that's what took you so long—am I right, darling? And who were you telephoning?" she said, her voice uninflected by teasing or annoyance, a mild voice and not without its charm.

"Wife," my friend said, tilting slightly forward with the utterance and then sagging back into his chair again.

And then he slid all the way off it.

I happened to be nearest, and was accordingly the one obliged to hoist him from the floor and get him settled again. But the man was jerking me down by my garment, and I suppose I was the only one to hear him. After all, he could barely speak above a whisper now. As a matter of fact, the others were no longer paying him any mind. Indeed, they seemed to have revisited the topic of urban devastations, and to be exploiting it with some delight.

"Sick. Come get me home. Wife," the silly tick said.

"Not *really*, lad," I said. "You say you called your *wife*? You told her to come take you home? To come *here*?"

But his only word to me was more of the same.

"Wife," my best friend said.


I was ready when the felon came. Doubtless, he presumed that improvising would throw me off, his randomizing the weekdays

and the hours that he cleaned. Certainly he could not have anticipated that I too could keep to an indeterminate routine, varying
the time I departed for the office, the time I returned home,
never repeating my behavior three days in a row. Make no mistake of it, I am not without my guile.

I was ready.

I could hear him down there, struggling to climb the steps to
the second landing, no doubt straining with the weight and bulk
of the lumpish vacuum cleaner that he used. I had never seen the
machine and I had never seen him, but I imagined that both
were big—very large, perhaps. That is why I had the hammer in
my hand when I opened the door to take up my station at the
top of the marble stairs.

Of course he left off coming when he saw me.

He lowered the machine to free himself of his burden, a brilliant
red canister very like a decorative oil drum, the thick hose looped
around his squat dark neck a serpent of a kind, a very serpent.

"What do you want?" he said.

"The sled," I said.

"Sled?" he said. "I have no sled."

He was not a big man.

I am not a big man. But he was not big, either—or so it
seemed sighting along the diagonal line that ran from me down
to him. And he was old. Sixty or more. Not that one could
know with people of his kind.

"You criminal," I said, and raised the hammer to make certain he saw I meant business.

"You're crazy!" he shouted up at me from where he with no-ticeable awkwardness stood.

"Crazy?" I screamed. "You call me crazy?"

I took two steps down.

He responded by shoving the vacuum cleaner against the iron railing and jamming it there with his knee.

"You're crazy!" he shouted again. "Leave me alone or I tell!"

"*Whom* will you tell?" I screamed. "It is I who will tell! I will tell them that you called me crazy! I will tell, you filth! I will tell that you called the father of a boy crazy! I will tell them that if I am crazy, it is you that made me crazy! Filth! Dirt!" I shrieked. "Go get the sled from wherever you put it or I will give you this!"

I held the hammer higher.

He let go of the vacuum cleaner and it slammed all the way down, its sullen descent thunderous as the steel barrel bashed the marble all the distance to the bottom.

He was quick for a man of his years, huffing up the stairs with bewildering speed. I hardly had a moment to ready myself, to swing with the force that was needed.

I hit him. I hit him in the face.

I think it was a solid blow.


I had just got my friend upright in his chair again when the woman that was coming toward us called out. She called loud enough for everyone to hear.

"I'll take him!" she called, and all the diners turned to gaze, gape, wait.

It would be a scene that everyone could enjoy, the theater that is implicit in every public setting.

You know what I mean. We are all of us identical in this, too, in our preparation for disorder, in confidently readying ourselves for it to scatter the order that so astonishingly obtains. I for one am never impressed by the statistical increase in murder and assault, believing that whatever rules us and contains us and keeps us from obliterating everything in sight can never do so with our connivance for very long.

She came ahead, cutting a robust figure through the stilled tables, calling out to us as she came, "I'll take him! I'll take him!"

She would be the wife, I thought, and that is of course who she was.

I stood to make the introductions, and the other fellow, instructed by my courtesy, stood too.

"My name is," I began, all welcome. But her attention was well to the side of me.

"I don't care what your name is," she said, regarding first her husband and then the woman who was still seated. "I want to know what her name is."

The second woman wasted not an instant. She pushed back her chair and rose. "My name?" she said, her voice no less moderate than when she had said, "No one is safe." I recall thinking what a wonderfully controlled woman this is, the very thing of the legislative, the state. I recall thinking what it would be like to enter her bed, to be in receipt of feeling expressed with such temperance. I imagined it would be a congenial experience, reminding myself that reserve nothing can dismantle is immensely more arousing than is the inner beast made manifest. Is it this that taxes my fondness for my wife?

"My dear," the second woman said, "I am the person your husband had been sleeping with until a few brief weeks ago."

We have a new sled now—not a plastic one, but a product made of a kind of pressed-wood material, a composite perhaps. Still, it is a Flexible Flyer, and that's the top of the line. We bought it the next larger size.

I suppose we would have had to give up the old one, anyway. To be sure, my boy is growing.

I wonder what sort of disfigurement the custodian displays on his face. It was a ball-peen hammer and therefore the striking surface was round, a small knob at least a nose width across.

He still services the building according to some irregular schedule he has devised. But I have naturally returned to my usual habits, off and away at nine sharp, back at my door at six on the dot, except of course for Fridays and Wednesdays, when I fetch the laundry and the groceries home.

You may be wondering if I have taken to placing the larger sled in the hallway where the missing one was kept.

I have, as a matter of fact.

I understand from my wife that the fellow still complains when he comes to do the carpet. He wants that little oblong cleaned just like the rest—and he says he will not resituate a sled to do it.

My wife tells me the old fellow is very angry about our persisting failure to cooperate, that he is threatening to remove any and all obstructions that interfere with his work.

My wife tells me the custodian says we are insane to continue to provoke him like this. My wife tells me that this is what the man says—if it proves your disposition to believe what tales are told by such a woman.

# MISS

# SPECIALTY

---

S UPPOSE SOMEBODY did to you something like this to you.
Suppose they made out their Last Will and so forth so it says
they want for their wife, they want for her when she dies, to be
laid to rest alongside of where they are, whereas they want for
you, when you die, to be laid to rest over on the other side of her
and not anywhere on the other side of him. So what is your
opinion of this if this was your father? I would be interested to
hear people's opinion of this if this was their father. What about
it if somebody (your father) did something like this to you? Because the thing of it is, what would you do if they did? Would
you go try to do anything about it? Because what I don't get is
what could you do? Because suppose he died already and suppose then she did. Because then who would be left for you to go
argue with? So if this was what happened to you, what would
you go do about it, do you think? Would you go try to do something about it with the front office people in charge of the cemetery? Would you go try to see if you could talk them out of it?
But don't they probably have to go by the Last Will and so forth?

They can't just forget it, can they? I don't think the people in charge of a cemetery can just say forget it as far as a Last Will and so forth goes. Because I'm positive they can't. So you know what I think? I think you just have to go along with it. I think you probably just have to. I think you either go along with it or go get yourself laid to rest someplace else. Like in a whole different cemetery, for instance. But like which cemetery? Which place? I never thought of any other place. I always thought of only this place. I always thought of where the whole family is— the aunts, the uncles, and of you-know-who, for instance. So I don't know. I have to make up my mind. But how can I make up my mind if I don't know? Well, this is not the only question. There is another question on top of this question. Because my cousins keep writing to me as regards the tree. My cousins keep asking me what is my vote as regards the tree. They mean because of the shade. My cousins keep telling me pay attention because the tree is killing the grass because of the shade. But would you believe them if they told you? Why should you believe them just because they told you? They want you to take their word for it—but isn't it what people always do? Don't people always want you to take their word for it? Didn't I take his word for it? But look where it got me, taking his word for it. It got me her side, hers—whereas what's so wrong with his? What's the matter with me being on his? I'm not saying the tree's not killing the grass. I am just saying maybe it's just what they're saying. So how do I vote? Because it has to be a unanimous vote. The front office people won't do anything about anything unless it's a unanimous vote. I could ask them themselves as far as the tree. But where's the guarantee? Do I have any guarantee? They could say it's killing the grass just to get rid of the question. Aren't they probably fed up with the question? And what if they're in cahoots with my cousins? Because I keep being of two minds as far as this. I keep being of two minds as regards everything. I need an eye-witness. But where am I going to get an eye-witness? You know what I am between? I am between the devil and the deep blue sea. In my mind, in my mind, I keep looking at these questions and keep seeing me being nothing but between the devil and the deep blue sea. Why is everybody taking advantage of me? People have to stop taking advantage of me. Everybody should be more on the up-and-up with me. There could be plenty of grass. There could be grass galore. So whose idea of it is it as regards how much of grass is not grass enough? My cousins probably have their reasons. Don't people have their reasons? There is such a thing as people having reasons. You know what else? Let me tell you what else. There are people who have it in for trees. There are people who have it in for people and then go get them confused with trees. There are people who go look at trees and then get them mixed up with people. Then they go around having it in for a tree. They can't help themselves. It's a thing in their minds. You can't blame them for it. It's not their fault. It's like a sickness. They don't even know what they're doing even. It is deep in their brain. They act like they've got something against a tree, but it's really something they've got against people. But it's all unbeknownst to them because of how deep it goes down in the brain. I used to be like this. I used to be just like this myself. It's a normal human thing. It couldn't be a more normal more human thing. You think there wasn't once a tree like this for me? I am not ashamed to say it. It does not make me ashamed for me to say it. It's one of the most normal of human things for people. It's just the way a tree can look. But since when is it normal for a Last Will and so forth? It's no joke of just nature, either. Because we had a street with places of business and some of them were like people to you, the businesses. I'm serious. You think places of business are places of business, but doctors will tell you. They don't want to tell you, but they can tell you. It's why I'm making a list of them. So we will see what we will see. Just don't hold me to anything. I am making no promises. Go look for somebody else if you are looking for somebody to go paint themselves into a corner for you. I don't want to get involved in any binding alliances. I am well aware of the stumbling blocks. Others have fallen to the wayside before me. But then you stop and think. You get back on track again. In your mind, in your mind, you get a picture of Central Avenue. You don't let them get under your skin. You take them in stride. Where would the human race be if every-body threw up their hands the instant there was something not in stride? Just listen to this, for instance—Bea's Tea Room, Ros-alind Light, the Arida Shop, Bess Diloff, Miller's, Raeder's, Cas-cade Laundry, Ben's Associated, Simon's, Sakoff's, Dalsimer's, W. R. Grant's, Ruth Hatch, Kate Hite, Postur-Line, Sisteen, Miss Specialty, the bank, the bank, Peninsula Bank. Go check on me if you want to go check on me. I don't care if you go check on me. I invite you to go check on me. I am extending you a written invitation for you to go check on me. Do you think I'm making a mountain out of a molehill! You think I'm making a mountain out of a molehill? Because I don't want for you to think I wouldn't respect your opinion. As far as your opinion, let's not forget whose idea it was for me to ask you for it in the first place. Because it was my idea for me to ask you for it in the first place. So what's the verdict? You think I should just learn to live with it? You think I should just chalk it up to experience and learn to live with it? Except what about what she once said to me once? Because how was I supposed to know anything about daffodils? I didn't know anything about daffodils. Nobody had ever taken me aside and said anything to me about daffodils. It was an unbeknownst subject to me, daffodils. There wasn't anybody who ever had given me any instruction along the lines of daffodils. Saying to a child who the fuck are you for you to go stand in my daffodils. For shame! You hear me? For shame! Whereas I thought all I was doing was just being under a tree. I thought look at me just being under this bad tree. Because this was the tree which looked like him to me, which looked like her to me, which looked like everybody to me. And she's screaming at me about daffodils. So I ask you, this is why I ask you, who can be laid to rest, how can anybody ever be laid to rest, you think I can ever be laid to rest—you or me or anyone ever?

# EATS WITH LENTRICCHIA AND OZICK

I AM WRITING this the night of 30 January 1994.

Barbara is in the next room.

She is being fed by two nurses. One spoons the soupy food onto Barbara's tongue, the other promptly pushes between Barbara's lips the canula that carries what Barbara cannot swallow down into the canister where what has already been suctioned out of Barbara's mouth is stored until someone must come dump the contents into the bedroom toilet so that the procedure might be continued without spill-over or mechanical breakdown.

Barbara will be fed, in this manner, all night, which means, as a rule—all night, that is—until about three in the morning, at which time Barbara will be prepared for bed, and then finally laid down onto it at about six-thirty. She will be gotten up from bed and positioned back into her chair at about nine-thirty, whereupon the feeding will begin again throughout the day and the night again, this in the care of two shifts of a pair of nurses—until about three in the morning of 31 January—if, in fact, there is going to be a 31 January this year.

I don't know.

I turn sixty in February.

I mention these matters not to press you with the force of conditions now in sway in Barbara's life but instead to create the context for the one literary memoir—if this might be claimed is what this recollection of mine is—I am ever likely to impart to print.

It concerns the critic Frank Lentricchia and the novelist Cynthia Ozick.

It concerns eating.

It concerns an item that belonged to Barbara but which I took from her—actually, from the chifferobe in the room she now sits in now eating in as I now sit writing in this one—the evening last July that Lentricchia and Ozick asked me to come out to dinner with them.

It was, the item, vintage spectacles that pinch the nose to keep themselves stationed at their post and that have a ribbon that, looped through an eyelet formed from the frame, goes over the head and takes purchase around the neck and hangs down.

Pince-nez, yes?

Barbara never wore them.

The glass in them was plain glass.

I had picked up this novelty for Barbara from some sort of fashion emporium back when we were first setting up housekeeping together.

The pince-nez were like so many of the things I was then

snatching from everywhere for Barbara—notions I had, frantic notions, of ornamenting her in her beauty.

Barbara was a very beautiful woman.

Barbara is still, inexpressibly, incredibly—reduced even to a depletion more severe than anything I would have imagined possible without death present in complete dominion—a very beautiful woman. You can see this, Barbara's authority in this category, registering in the styles of approach made to her by the young women who come to nurse Barbara—a sort of recognition, I think it is: a sort of satisfied acknowledgment of the insult nature reserves—justly!—for the very beautiful.

Barbara is regnant in there in our bedroom with two such nurses right now. They feed her, or struggle to feed her, as Barbara, for her part, struggles to swallow little sips of what was yesterday cooked and pureed for her, everybody in there, none more blindly than Barbara herself, getting a good look at what most of us never see: the work that can be done to the body by amyotropic lateral sclerosis.

Lou Gehrig's Disease.

But I was telling you about another experience in eating and about other persons—and about the pince-nez.

Which last I had taken from the top drawer of Barbara's chifferobe in order that I might feel I was in prospect of holding my own—as a full-fledged participant—in the company of Lentricchia and Ozick the night of the dinner I am remarking.

I took them with me, the pince-nez, for just that reason—or for no reason that I can honorably say.

I don't know.

Say that I had been in all day, been in for days, had not been out of the house—not at night, anyway—for weeks and weeks—and had certainly not been out of the house at night for anything social in months, months, months.

They—Lentricchia and Ozick—phoned, said come out to dinner with us, said come meet us in an hour at The Grand Ticino, said come look for it just north of Bleecker on Thompson.

I said yes, yes, oh yes, hung up the phone, went with tears in my eyes—it's crazy—to the bedroom, to the chifferobe, took out the pince-nez, got my shoe trapped under one of the canulas or catheters or electric cords everywhere underfoot, got the shoe loose, went to the bookshelves, took down Ozick's *Bloodshed*, took down Lentricchia's *Ariel and the Police*, went to the kitchen, made out a note for the nurses then on duty and for those to come on at ten, said I'd be back no later than eleven, added the telephone number where I could be reached, and went, left, fled, took myself out into the street in the temper of one released.

Now the anecdote.

What I know I called a memoir but can now see never will accumulate itself into anything so grand, and God knows into nothing anywhere on speaking terms with something traveling under papers as a literary one:

It's just a bit.

I can tell it to you, the whole bit, in no time flat.

They were late.

I sat there being exasperated with them. Why were they late? Wasn't I on time? What right did they have to be late when there I was, right when they said I should be—on fucking time? And what right did they have to make it up between them that we, the three of us, would come eat at The Grand Ticino when—fuck, fuck!—doors away, also just north on Thompson off Bleecker, was Porto Bello—where with Bloom, with Donoghue, with Ozick, with Lentricchia—with Barbara, goddamn it!—I had had such good times, such happinesses—releases to, not releases from.

I tried thinking of topics.

Then I was glad of it, glad for it—glad the dirty rats were late.

Because I did not have anything to talk with them about—no topics, not a topic—did not have anything to say for myself, did not feel anything in me sufficient in worth to swap for the gift of anyone's time with me—except to hand these people my tears again in thanks again for their thinking again to ask me to come out with them again for eats.

I had the one topic.

Barbara.

Barbara dying.

So I sat there being exasperated a little bit, and weeping a little bit, and being pleased with myself for the pince-nez hanging zanily from my neck and for the copy of *Bloodshed* and for the copy of *Ariel and the Police* I had thought to pack along with me for no motive I could state to you with anymore good sense backing it up than I could summon in defense of myself for my getting myself up with the pince-nez.

I thought: Tell them I'd just made up my mind my favorite sentence is Edward Loomis's "Mary Rollins was born in a high white frame house shaded by elms."

I thought: Tell them I'm getting ready to make my second-favorite sentence "The icepack has melted and the American River is running fast."

I thought: Do I tell them it's mine, this sentence—ah, shit, compound sentence!—or tell them instead that all I really did was steal it from where it was scribbled up on some wall somewhere?

I thought: Tell them I've got money in my pocket and I'm going to get bad drunk and then get on a bus going north.

I thought: Tell them I'm pretty damn burnt-up they didn't deal me in when they didn't settle on Porto Bello.

I thought: Tell them they're my first- and my second-best friends?

I sat there thinking.

I sat there thinking, sat there waiting, sat there making believe I was actually reading the books I had laid out in my lap when I had pushed back my chair back away from the table when the waiter had come and had put a cup of espresso in front of me and had filled the bread basket with some great-looking bread in it for me and had poured out for me a little dish of olive oil for me, and had, in every ordinary thing the fellow had done for me, in every conventional ministration the waiter had enacted for me, that the man had—the strictness, the covenant with protocol—got the tears to come from me again, delivered me to a sort of small weeping again—so that, sure, sure, I guess I could not actually have sat there reading anything even if I had actually been trying to.

I sat there thinking: Hey, what do they make of me, the other people back behind me in this place, me, this pose-taker I am, this show-person sitting here, the ridiculous specs stuck to the nose, the broad black grosgrain ribbon swagged martially across the chest, the legs arranged at a grand three-quarter torque, the auspicious-looking books laid out in the lap, the chair shoved back away from the table in an exhibition of a sort of magisterial remove?

I sat there thinking: Where the fuck are they, the dirty rats, not to be here now, not for them to see me looking like this, not for them to be here right this instant coming up on me seeing me looking like this? I'm ready! I'm ready!—ready to be viewed!—but are the bastardos here and ready, set, go! to do it?

I sat thinking: Tell them about how on my way downtown I spotted on Broadway between Twenty-second and Twenty-first a store called "Gordon" with a sign saying something like *Sells Tricks, Sells Novelties, Sells Disguises*.

I thought: Tell them they're both my first-best friends.

I thought: Tell them they made me cry.

I thought: Tell them everything has been making me cry.

I thought: Tell them I put on a dirty movie when Barbara was sleeping or when I thought Barbara was sleeping and there was a girl in it getting it from all sides but who never once looked at any of the ones giving it to her but instead was only always looking off somewhere away from everything going on in the holes in her body as if—in a gaze, in a gaze!—she was looking into the mists of paradise?

I thought: Tell them, of the three chairs, that of the three chairs, that I, Gordon, was the first one here first but that I, Gordon, of the three chairs, that I took the one chair facing to the back, took the one chair facing to the kitchen, because what wouldn't I, Gordon, do for my two best friends if not eat shit for them, if not face the kitchen doing it for them?

I thought: Tell them I took the pince-nez when Barbara wasn't looking, tell them I never told Barbara I was taking them, tell them I couldn't really read with them, tell them I wasn't really reading with them, tell them they didn't have anything but just plain glass in them, tell them I'm not going to be ashamed of any of this, tell them I'm not going to be ashamed of this or of anything anywhere to do with any of this, tell them no, no, not if at least, if I, Gordon, can be somewhere on time when I am god-damn told to be and they—the bastardos!—can't!

In the midst of which consideration I take up a big piece of the bread up from the bread basket and tear off a little piece of it from the big piece and put the little piece down into the little dish of olive oil and soak the little piece of bread with olive oil and then take up the salt shaker and salt the oiled bread with salt and put the little piece of salted, oiled bread into my mouth and start chewing and keep chewing and then take up the cup of espresso and take a sip from the cup of espresso and sit chewing and chewing and posing and posing and making-believe I am reading but sit really actually just thinking—fuck, fuck—this fucking bread here is pretty fucking good bread here, this bread here at The Grand Ticino is pretty fucking good bread here— and just getting more bread, getting it all salted, getting it all oiled, getting more of the coffee into my mouth, getting the whole gob of it all good and chewed and soaked and mashed, thinking, thinking: Tell the bastardos what, what, what?

I think: Proust!

I think: That's it, Proust!

What a topic, Proust!—the bum, the dirty rat, the bastardo braggart forgetting the cookie, and whose damn cookie is it but his own damn cookie!

Tell them the filth can't even damn remember to remember his own damn cookie, can't even damn remember not even three little pages hence concerning remembering, concerning *remembering*, goddamn it, that it's the two of them, that it's the totality of the two of them, that it is the totalitarian unicity of the blend of savors that authorizes the emancipation of anything, that it's the tea and the cookie, that it's the two of them, the tea now, the cookie now, the both of them now, this reciprocation.

Tell them I think.

Tell them the instant they show up that I think.

And then I think Holy God Jesus, how about asphyxiation for a topic!

Because it is all of a sudden occurring to me that I am fucking goddamn sitting here in The Grand Ticino *strangling*!

I mean it, I mean it, I've fucking gone and got a lump of oily salty coffee-ed-up mush that's gone and got itself caught halfway down and won't go anymore down than halfway down anymore because there is laid out under it this swag of big broad black grosgrain I somehow got caught in under the bread when I was sticking the fucking bread in my mouth and then got the ribbon halfway swallowed down under the bread and it's hung up on me halfway down, like a bundle of it, like a bag of it, and it won't, the whole killing sack of it, it won't come back up because it's gone too far down for it to do it and it won't go all the way down because my neck's got it by a rope and will not let it go.

And I think: Idiot, idiot, quick, quick!—act fast before you have suffocated yourself!—either yank and rip out your teeth out or see if you can swallow your head!

That's the thought I thought.

I don't know for how long.

All I know is, hey, Barbara knows.

Legs still crossed in posed pose, books—books!—still exhibited upon my person—while death hurries to do an honest job of it from the props bullshitting furnished.

Okay, so that's the literary part.

The memoir part is did I or didn't I sit here and not forget that it was all of them, all?

Oil, salt, coffee, ribbon, bread.

Six, actually—actually the components constituting the effect, don't they come, all in all, to six?

The swift convergence, fluent—calamity!—everything in your gullet at once—I can count at least to six. And what about eyelet?—and vanity?—and canula? But it's swell by me if you and the critic and you and the novelist want to take the list anywhere off and away into the mists of rhymes and schemes.

Except just don't ever go accusing anybody of ever being anything too Prousty, deal?

I said it, my darling—didn't I?

Didn't I just—him, your husband—say deal?

# HISTORY, OR THE
# FOUR PICTURES
# OF VLUDKA

———————

H E SAID that he had been considering the convention of
the Polish girl, and I said, "In literature—you mean in
literature," and he said, "Yes, of course," how else would he
mean? touching eyeglasses, beard, lip while noting that he was
feeling himself compelled to take up the pose of the poet in
eucharistic recollection of etc., etc., etc.—as literary necessity,
that is.

He said, "So can you help, do you think?"

I said, "From memory, you mean."

"That's it," he said. "Any Polish girl you ever had yourself
any sort of a thing with."

I can tell you what the trouble with me was—no beard anywhere on me, no eyeglasses either, meat of real consequence to
neither of my lips—nothing, at least, to speak of, nothing to give
me a good grab of anything, nothing on my face for anyone to
hang onto, nothing to offer a good grip to even myself.

He said, "Whatever comes to mind, I think."

Here was the thing with me—I did not know what to do with my hands.

"Whatever pops into your head," he said, off and at it again, fingering eyeglasses, beard, lip.

The lout was all feelies, I tell you—the lummox was ledges from stem to stern.

"So," he said, "anything you might want to conjure up for me, then? I mean, just the barest sketching, of course, no need for names and, as it were, addresses."

But I had never had one. I mean, I hadn't had a Polish girl. What I had had back before that inquiry had come to me was a great wanting to pass myself off as a fellow who had had whatever could be got.

"Vludka," I said, "her name was Vludka."

"Wonderful," he said. He said, "Name's Vludka, you say."

"Yes," I said, "and very, for that matter, like it, too."

"I see her," her said. "Stolid Vludka."

"In the extreme," I said. "In manner and in form."

"Yes, the nakedness," he said. "A certain massiveness, I imagine—wide at the waist, for instance, the effect of the body built up in slabs."

I said, "Vludka's, yes. And hard it was, too. Oh, she was tougher and rougher than I was, of course—morally and physically the bigger, better party."

"But smallish here," he said, showing.

I said, "Even said she was sorry about it for the way they were before she took her clothes off, and then when she had them off, saw that what she should have been warning me about was about how big everything else was."

He said, "Could tell you'd be lost inside her, awash in stolid Vludka, splinter proposing monkey business to lumberyard."

I said, "There I was, a punk in spirit, a puniness in fiber."

He said, "It was impossible."

"I said to her, 'Vludka, this is impossible.'"

He said, "She was too Polish for you, much too Polish."

"So I said to her, 'Do something, Vludka. Manage this for us.'"

He said, "She was pliant, compliant—Polish. You said to her, 'You handle it, Vludka, and I'll watch,' and she did," he said, "didn't she?"

"Because she was pliant," I said. "Compliant," I said. "Polish," I said.

He said, "It took her eleven minutes."

I said, "I sort of knew it would."

He said, "That's how stolid she was."

I said, "It was endless. My arm was exhausted for her. I timed her on my watch. Even for a Polish girl, it was incredible. I tell you, she used a blunt fingertip, a thumb even."

"It was ponderous," he said. "Thunderous," he said. "You thinly watching, you meagerly urging, 'For pity's sake, come, Vludka, come!'"

What I didn't tell him is that what I was really watching were the four pictures of Vludka on Vludka's bedroom wall instead.

These are what they were of—of Vludka at the railing of a big wooden-looking boat, of Vludka in a toy runabout with her hands up on the wheel, of Vludka with others on a blanket in a forest, of Vludka squatting on a scooter near a road sign that when Vludka finished doing it to herself she said, "Majdanek, you know what's there? Or was?"

He said, "Well?"

I said, "Well what?"

He said, "What you were thinking—the road sign—Majdanek—what was it that was there?"

I said, "You read my mind."

He said, "No. Just the standard stuff about the camps."

All my life I have never known what to do with my hands. Except for shit like this.

# LEOPARD IN
# A TEMPLE

------

LOOK, let's make it short and sweet. Who anymore doesn't go crazy from overtures, from fanfares, from preambles, from preliminaries? So, okay, here is the thing—this is my Kafka story, fine and dandy. Actually, it is going to be my against-Kafka story. Because what I notice is you have to have a Kafka story one way or the other. So this is my Kafka story, only it is going to be one which is against Kafka. Which is different from being against Kafka's *stories*, although I would probably be against those, too, if I ever went back and really reread any of them.

I'm not interested.

It's exclusively the man himself which I am interested in.

But not to the extent that I would give you two cents for him even if he was made of money, which is what I understand the man in his lifetime was.

I'll tell you about lifetimes.

I have a person here who is a kindergartner, so right there this takes care of lifetimes. Whereas I don't have to tell you that what Kafka got was *nafkelehs*.

You say this Kafka knew a lot. But show me where it says he knew from doily-cutters.

Or even what cutters were who didn't work in paper.

Take my dad, for the most convenient comparison.

The man couldn't make a go of it in business.

In other words, so far as his fortunes went, if dry goods was hot, then he was in wet ones.

But who has the energy for so much history?

Kafka, on the other hand, the rascal doesn't even know the meaning of the word idle, that's how fast he sits himself down to write his own father a letter. But let me ask you something? You want to read to me from the book where it says this letter-writer ever had the gall to also say as much as boo to his mother?

Save your breath.

I am not uninformed as to the character of the author.

Pay attention—we are talking about a creature who could not wait to stab the son of a butcher in the back—but where is it on exhibit that this Kafka Schmafka ever had the belly to split an infinitive even in his own language?

Now take me and my mother, to give you two horses of a different human color.

You know what?

We neither of us ever had one.

Or even a pony they came and rented you.

You see what I am saying to you? Because I am saying to you that nothing is out-of-bounds so far as I myself am personally concerned—unless it is something which is so dead and buried that I have got nothing to gain from unearthing it, which she, the old horseless thing, doesn't happen to be yet.

But Kafka, so how come wherever you turn, it's Kafka, Kafka—just because brushing his own teeth, the man couldn't help himself, the toothbrush alone could make him vomit?

You know what I say?

I say this Kafka had it too good already, a citizen in good standing in the Kingdom of Bohemia, whereas guess who gets to live out his unpony-ed life in the United States of unprincely America?

In a mixed building.

In even an apartment which is mixed also.

With a kindergartner—who is meanwhile, by the way, looking to me not just like the bug he looked to me like when he came into this world but also more and more like he is turning into a person who could turn big and normal and dangerous.

You want to hear something?

In kindergarten, they teach reading already. So the teacher makes them make a doily and then lay it down over some Kafka and recite through the holes to her.

This day and age!

These modern times!

Listen, I also woke up in my room once, and guess what.

Because the answer is I was still no different.

From head to toe, I had to look at every ordinary inch of what I took to bed with me.

Hey, you want to hear something?

I was *un*metamorphosed!

You look like I look, you think you get a Felice? Because the answer is that you do not even get a Phyllis.

Fee-lee-chay.

"Oh, Feeleechay, my ancestor is a barbarian, a philistine, a businessman—so lose not a moment, my pretty, if you are for art, suck my dick this instant!"

But, to be fair, my mother used to say klee-yon-tell.

Still does, I bet.

You know what I bet? I bet if I ever could get my mother on the telephone, you know what she would say to me? The woman would say to me, "Sweetheart, you should come down here to visit me down here, because they cater down here to the finest kleeyontell."

One time I went to call her up once, went to look for her number once, but never did it, never did.

Had to scream bloody-murder in my office instead.

Hate to admit it, but I did.

Boy oh boy, was that a scream.

From flipping around the Rolodex cards and then from seeing what was on her card when the flipped-around cards fell open to hers.

You know what I say?

Who wishes the man ill? But I would like to see him wake up to what I wake up to.

Just once.

Forget it.

The rogue was small potatoes.

My dad lived through fifty years as a cutter in girls' coats, whereas Kafka, the sissy, could not even shape up and live through his own life.

But why argue?

Where's the percentage?

It wasn't a cockroach on my mother's card.

It was just a groggy earwig instead.

# EVERYTHING

# I KNOW

---

THE WIFE INSISTED she would tell her version first. I was instantly interested because of the word.

The husband stood by in readiness. Or perhaps his version still needed to be tinkered with.

She took a breath, grinned, and got right to the most alarming part first. At least to what she wished us—and the husband?—to regard as the part that had most alarmed her.

She said she waked to find a man in her bed. Not the husband, of course. The husband, she said, was next door, visiting with a friend. She said the husband often did this, spent the evening hours visiting, next door or somewhere else. At any rate, the wife said she did not scream because fear had made her speechless. She said that speechlessness was a common enough reaction, and to this the husband nodded in enthusiasm.

But she was able to get to her feet and run. She ran out the front door. She said she ran three blocks to a telephone booth and called the police.

"My God," I said. "That's terrifying."

"I know," she said, and smiled.

I took her smile to be a common enough reaction.

I said, "And you were so terrified that you ran away from the house with the man and your little boy still in it?"

"Isn't it amazing?" the wife said. "That's how scared you can get."

"You don't need to tell me," I said. "But just think."

"Oh," she said, "they're not interested in kids."

The husband took a breath, and then made his way into his version, not one word about which part was the worst.

He said he came in by the back door, exercising great care to quiet the key because it was, after all, late. He said he did likewise with the action of his tread. But then he saw the front door wide open—and so he stepped swiftly to the little boy's room, and saw the little boy safe in his bed.

"You see?" the wife said.

I said, "Thank God."

"I went to our bedroom next," the husband said.

He said he saw the bed empty and the bathroom door closed.

"Good God," I said, "the rapist is in there!"

My wife said, "For goodness sake, let *him* tell it."

The husband said he went weak with shock. He said he understood it was useless to stand there exhorting himself to open the bathroom door. He said he was simply certain of it—the wife would be in there, dead.

"Can you blame him?" the wife said.

The husband said, "So I sat down on the bed and called the police."

Then they both smiled.

"The rapist wasn't in there?" I said.

*"Please,"* my wife said.

The husband said he could barely speak. He said the police kept urging him to speak up.

"My wife's missing!"

This is what the husband said he screamed into the telephone, but that the police said no, not to worry, that his missus was in a phone booth just blocks from the house.

"That's awful," my wife said.

I said, "But the bathroom."

The husband said, "I didn't touch that door until the police got there—and when they did, of course it was empty."

"Of course," I said. "Is there a window in there?"

The wife nodded.

"Open," the husband said, satisfied.

"That's the way he got out," the wife efficiently added.

"The rapist," my wife said in just as quick succession.

I've told you everything I know. I've told it to you precisely as it was revealed to me. But there is something in these events that I don't understand. I think there is something that those two people—no, three—aren't telling me. I sometimes think it must be staring me right in the face, just the way the three of them were when the story was all finished.

# THE FOREIGNER
# AS APPRENTICE

---

YOU DO NOT BELIEVE ME. Why won't you believe me? Whose vengeance is it that keeps cursing me for my making an ever more extravagant investment in what's to be made over to me from my more and more telling all? I am neither liked nor believed—or did I just lay down a plank of past-participializing wrong-way-wise from left to right? No matter, Gordo's busted—left behind by wife and child, naught left for him to do for himself but rattle around in search of gash and/or gash and romance. And so it was that I was able to form a yeasty introduction to a woman who had made plain that she was Susan.

Or had said Susanne.

No matter—the matter was settled with dispatch—the practiced considerations ensuing at all modest speed—a brief tea at a tearoom excessively dainty enough, a not unmodulated vehemence of ardors passing from one to the other by telephone— and, with charming promptitude, the whole of it, concluded— to wit, that Susan or Susanne would come with herself to my place to a small supper that I would serve to her, and, if all appeared to go acceptably, not remove herself therefrom until an hour in the morning.

And so it was that I was, on a certain afternoon, making my way along the avenue to first fetch and then carry home with me a kind of stylish bread in support of my arrangements to encourage this outcome. Well, I was weeping as I went. I do often do this—weep some—chiefly—no, entirely—when I am out-of-doors and mainly in motion, as of course one is when one walks. I mean to say to you that I seemed to myself to be weeping—but whether this effect results from a feeling that is unbeknownst to me seizing me or from eye tissue punished by the cruel vapors of our streets, how am I to be the one to know?

Tears occur in me.

Are an occurrence in me.

Were then occurring in me as I went making my way along the avenue for the bread—and would doubtless occur in me, be a homeward reoccurrence in me, would presently be recurring in me as I went coursing back up the avenue for home and for the woman Susan—or would it be for Susanne?

But I was tearless when taking the loaf that I wanted from the basket where all the loaves, in invitation, were presented all of the way up on end.

Tearless, too, when preparing myself to turn to give money to the young thing at the cash register.

Tearless, three, when I heard "Mr. Lish, is it?"

I said to no face that I could see: "Sorry?"

But then there was a face, all right, and from it there issued a revision: "You're Mr. Lish, are you not?"

I had had to move the bread from one hand to the other to use my customarily favored hand to be ready with the money—and so the bread seemed to me, given the locus of the hand that held it and the less grace that hand was able to do this work with—to be rudely prodding the space that was now assembling itself between my accuser and myself.

"Please"—it was the voice again—"it's been years. But you must, you must, you must be Mr. Lish."

It was a woman.

Uninteresting eyes, sadly too interesting eyeglasses, spectacles established pugnaciously forward on a nose never meant to sustain even a small sneeze.

I wiped at my eyes.

I had the money in the hand that did it.

It did no good.

I used my knuckles to wipe at the cloudier eye harder. "I'm very sorry," I said. "You seem to know me," I said. "It's the snow," I said. "I'm just on an errand," I said. "This bread," I said, now giddily conscious of my bearing the ficelle as if about to poke at her chest with it.

"Yes," she said. "Snow is so disconcerting, isn't it?" she said. "It's lovely when it first falls—but now look at it—just slush and dirt and wretchedness, wretchedness," she said.

"Yes," I said. "One's shoes," I said. "They get to look so awful," I said.

"Wear boots," she said. "I wear boots," she said.

"Of course," I said, and got the bread out from between us even though I did not want to take food into the hand that held money. "Let me just pay for this," I said.

"Oh, but you don't remember me," the woman said.

"I'm sorry," I said. "Sometimes the snow," I said.

"I'm Harris Drewell's mother," the woman said.

"Yes," I said. "You are Harris Drewell's mother," I said.

"Harris Drewell," the woman said, and I could see that what she had in her arms were several loaves of a different style of bread. "A classmate of your boy's at school."

"Well, of course," I said, and the thought rushed through me that she had taken for herself a kind of bread that might better have accomplished my aim with Susan.

Or with Susanne.

"Mr. Lish," the woman said, "I just want to say for Mr. Drewell and myself that we are all of us very sorry for your un-happiness. And for Harris, too, you understand—Harris would offer his sympathies too, you understand."

"Oh, well," I said, "this snow, you know. Can you counte-nance it? Can you ever?" I said, and struggled to swing myself around a little so as to, by so doing, give evidence to all con-cerned that the person at the cash register could not, for one more instant, be kept waiting for her to have payment.

"He's gone with the Foreign Service, you know. It's just an internship, of course. He's just an intern, of course. But we're all of us "of course" very proud of him, Harris."

"As am I," I said, and gave to the clerk the money and got back from her the coins that were coming to me and then made—my vision awash with confusion, confusion, avalanche, wallow—for the door.

"Oh, they'll be back, Mr. Lish—have no fear of it, have none!" I heard the woman call to me, but thought, once I had gotten myself back onto the sidewalk and again onto my course, thought no, no, I had imagined it, I must have just imagined it, that what she had instead said was, "Wear boots, you imp, for pity's sake—boots!"

It was a block or so onward that I could recall my sometimes seeing this person when I had escorted my child to school and had stood about with the fathers and mothers and more often the nannies and chauffeurs in such hopeful assembly.

"My God, Harris Drewell's mother," I called out to myself as I went.

For hadn't I once begged the gods for them to please give me Harris Drewell's mother please for me just to once please fuck?

I am telling.

This is the truth that I am telling.

Just as I am telling that I was making up my mind not for me to get out my shoe polish and clean off my shoes, that I was making up my mind, had, had, just as I was turning off the avenue to go the rest of the distance for the corner and home, made up my mind not ever again for me to clean off my shoes not for this Susan nor for this Susanne or for anyone, but instead to get her fair share of the bread into her and of everything else spread out for her into her—potage, silage, rump!—as fast as it all could be decently gotten into her and then to get rid of her and then rid of everybody—of every other else.

So there's the proof for you.

Don't you see it's only a fool who tells a story that is true?

Even the names, by Christ—the very names!—come out looking—nay, crying aloud—false, false, false.

# FEAR:
# FOUR EXAMPLES

---

M Y DAUGHTER called from college. She is a good student, excellent grades, is gifted in any number of ways.

"What time is it?" she said.

I said, "It is two o'clock."

"All right," she said. "It's two now. Expect me at four—four by the clock that said it's two."

"It was my watch," I said.

"Good," she said.

It is ninety miles, an easy drive.

At a quarter to four, I went down to the street. I had these things in mind—look for her car, hold a parking place, be there waving when she turned into the block.

At a quarter to five, I came back up.

I changed my shirt. I wiped off my shoes. I looked into the mirror to see if I looked like someone's father.

She presented herself shortly after six o'clock.

"Traffic?" I said.

"No," she said, and that was the end of that.

After dinner, she complained of insufferable pains, and doubled over on the dining-room floor.

"My belly," she said.

"What?" I said.

She said, "My belly. It's agony. Get me a doctor."

There is a large and famous hospital mere blocks from my apartment. Celebrities go there, statesmen, people who must know what they are doing.

With the help of a doorman and an elevator man, I got my child to the hospital. Within minutes, two physicians and a corps of nurses took the matter in hand.

I stood by watching.

It was hours before they had her undoubled and were willing to announce their findings.

A bellyache, a rogue cramp, a certain unspecifiable seizure of the intestine—vagrant, unamusing, but not worth the bother of further inquiry.

We left the hospital unassisted, using a chain of tunnels in order to shorten the distance home. The exposed distance, that is—since it would be four in the morning on the city streets, and though the blocks would be few, each one of them would be a challenge. So we made our way along the system of underground passages that link the units of the hospital, this until we were forced to surface and exit. We came out onto a street with not a person on it—until I saw him, a man who was going from car to car. He carried something under his arm. It looked to be a furled umbrella—but it could not have been what it looked to be. No, no, it had to have been a tool of entry disguised as something innocent.

He turned to us as we stepped along, and then he turned back to his work—loitering at the automobiles, trying the doors, and sometimes using the thing to dig at the windows.

"Don't look," I said.

My daughter said, "What?"

I said, "There's someone across the street. He's trying to jimmy open cars. Just keep on walking as if you don't see him."

My daughter said, "Where? I don't see him."

I put my daughter to bed and the hospital charges on my desk, and then I let my head down on the pillow and listened.

There was nothing to hear.

Before I surrendered myself to sleep, there was only this in my mind—the boy in the treatment room across the corridor from my daughter's, how I had wanted to cry out each time he had cried out as a stitch was sutured into his hand.

"Take it out! Take it out!"

This is what the boy was shrieking as the surgeon labored to close the wound.

I thought about the feeling in me when I had heard that awful wailing. The boy wanted the needle out. I suppose the needle hurt worse than the wound the needle would close. Then I considered the statement for emergency services, translating the amount first into theater tickets, then into hand-ironed shirts.

# FANGLE
# OR FIRE

---

P EOPLE BELIEVE ME, or think me, imagine me to be Lish, the lit-fag, hyphen entered aforethought. Whereas nothing could be farther—or further—from the truth. The truth is that I have not been, and shall never be, a man of books, as I have, whilst under orders, sought to seem to be, but that I have been— and should like to continue to be—a fighter against our nation's enemies within the theater of our nation's boundaries. I was inducted into service in 1954, this at an installation called Miami Retreat. My sponsor was Helen Deutsch, married name Siegel, younger sister to my mother, Regina. I can furnish the documents. You have heard of Fort George Meade? You have heard of Maryland's Laurel Park? You have heard of the National Security Agency? The terms of the agency's mandate to act for the common good, as inaugurated by the President and as thereafter regulated solely under the direct jurisdiction of the Joint Chiefs of Staff, frees the N.S.A., shall we call it, from potentialities of legal and political tether to all entities of Government save those just remarked. Hence, the volatility—or vaporousness—of my position and that of my colleagues—or cohorts. Please know that I seek to cover myself with no special status—or favor—when I hasten, as I must, to illumine a certain detail of my affiliation as heretofore recorded. The N.S.A., or NSA, was organized, as was everything else in its day, to perform duties contextualized within the perception of that which could properly be construed as international in the emphasis of concern, thus confining, to the extent reasonable, the compass of the aforementioned entity to activities whose source and flux placed the impress of those activities beyond the borders of this land—or suitably without the so-called Line of Limit. Here you have it. We come, in this, to the peculiar character of my status and, accordingly, to the case to be made for the making of this disclosure. Let me explain—or struggle to unstitch—what will at first appear, I do not doubt, both inexplicable and too tightly seamed to yield to parsing. My mother is—or was—Regina. She was one of five girls—daughters of Louis Deutsch and Ethel Goldstein. My father, however—and now we commence to approach the crux of it—was one of five boys and three girls—the offspring, it was claimed, of Rachel Boulansky and Isaac Lishkowitz. In fact, my paternal grandmother's name was Routchel Boolski, my paternal grandfather, for his part, named Sik Lescowicz. These two made their way to these shores, it was thought, from Russ-Polen, whereas papers demonstrate Louis and Ethel brought themselves hither from Vienna. The issue of this other pair—Pauline, Regina, Helen, Adele, and Sylvia, names cited in order of birth—spoke, owing to the fluency of their parents in these tongues—or idioms, or idioma—German and Hungarian and, presently, impeccable English, owing, the accomplishment of this last, to the intervention of the Metropolitan Orphan Asylum at Astoria, New York, the shelter to which the children were sent on the occasion of the death of Louis (circumstances "suspicious," to say the "least") and the ensuing incompetence of Ethel, herself confined to a facility for persons suffering such an infelicity. It was here—at Metropolitan—that (these details are acknowledged in diarist accounts given by Pauline, the eldest) the keen lingual and mathematical skills of Helen and Adele were first detected and thereafter, quite purposively, "cultivated," or nourished, or encouraged. That our forefathers were not unalert to the coming belligerencies with the Axis powers, this so long previous to the actual onset of events, is terribly interesting, or intriguing, I believe—or allege—but we doubtless could not handily sustain a digressive inquiry into the matter so soon in the formation of our not unperplexing considerations, could we? Thusly, thenly, as for the case in and among the non-Deutsch side of the "family," the products were these, sequence of enunciation again controlled by order of sequencing: Joseph, Jenny, Ida, Charles, Lily, Samuel, Philip, Henry. I now focus our attention on two suggestive items—no person named Uncle Joseph nor any person named Aunt Jenny was ever in view either of myself or of any official body in pursuit of the Government's proprietary engagement with the lives of its "citizens." Furthermore, Henry, my uncle Henry—all through the war years—which is to say the years one is referring to when one refers to the years of the war years—

"fished" for flounder and for fluke, this whilst anchored "off-shore" in the so-called channel, his vessel a small, wood boat—or wooden boat—or rowboat—its engine either a modestly pow-ered Johnson outboard motor, or Evinrude, or Mercury. The man's "sons"—Big Eugene, Kenny or Kenneth, and Abby or Abbott—were, during the interval to which I now point no-tice—members of our armed forces, this in the European theater of operation. Fulton Lewis Jr. would say, "That's the top of the news from here!" Here is a further element meriting, at this stage, I aver, or believe—or think—of notation—namely, that in the film, or in the motion picture, *The Memoirs of Vidouq*—which "theatrical" event I was witness to whilst conducting myself as a "book editor" (in the employ of the house of Alfred A. Knopf, an imprint of the corporate "body" known as Random House) and thus comporting myself as a participant, on behalf of the forego-ing, in or at the Frankfurt Book Fair of 1991—there appears a character called "the abbess." Need I say more? I think not. The piece was shown—or exhibited—at—mark you, please—the Prater Nonstop. The credits, offered for one and all at the finito of things—a black-and-white affair mounted, one gathered, sometime during, or just previous to, the hostilities so famously prosecuted across Europe by the "powers that be," or "powers that were"—declare one Sissy Mangan as the performer playing the part of "the abbess." I ask that you offer sensitive study to the name Sissy Mangan. You are, or are not, conversant, are you not, with the curious sentence "It is well for you"? You can, if inter-rogated on such a score, indicate the speaker of this sentence—

the distinguished text wherein the sentence is "spoken"? Let me, as a poseur, or posturer, or postulant, hurry to proclaim that I hope so. I cannot overstate the breadth of what I shall, in this "scription," expect of you—nor the finesse or vitesse or depth of it. I beg you to realize I "sign" my death warrant when I "sign" this writing. It must therefore not be in vain that I do so. Bear in mind, dearest, the sons of Uncle Henry are at large, absence of hyphen aforethought. Nevertheless, insofar as the existence of the commission treating of the resolution of relations between the Deutsches and the "Lishes" is at stake, there remain, or remains, the Chinese to contend with, do there, or does there, not? Am I losing you? Alas, what is it but regrettable that the tale to be told cannot be told elsewise? Yet told it must be. Yet go forward, as teller, I must and will. Adele is dead—"presumably" of cancer. A carcinoma of the bones, which probably hurts like the dickens. Like Regina—Reggie—Adele busied herself with covering various of her "garments" with sequins and beads. Or spangles. One such spangle—another detail it would "be well" for you to keep "in mind"—was known as the bugle, or bugler. But we must not abandon touch with the truth that these ornaments were obtained by Adele—and by Reggie—in great number, or supply— and without cost to themselves—by their exploiting their ties with the "Lish" side of the family, which "side" was reputedly, or reportedly, or putatively, in the hat business—and was therefore in the practice of buying trim in bulk. Dad—my father—would fetch such "matériel" home to Mother, who, for her part, would, in turn, fetch a lesser portion of same along to her sister Adele.

Helen, meanwhile, was "in" Laurel Park (Maryland), where, as of this writing, a certain Freedom Fighter and his spouse struggle to sustain their matrimony in (protected) residence. Helen, meanwhile—we are "talking about" the years 1937 and 1938—was "one of many," or was "one among many," which many—the plant at Fort George Meade was still to become fully operational—devoted itself, or themselves, to the round-the-clock collective expression of their singular gifts in an assault on the stubborn fascia, or raffia, of certain enemy codes, or of the codes of certain enemies. By 1954, or in the year of 1954, Helen Deutsch, then Helen Deutsch Siegel, stood forth, among her kind, as the premiere cryptoanalyst in Government service. She was "retired" from that service in the year 1962, this in possession of a lozenge-configured medal. Listen, she kept upon her person two pistols—a sidearm and chest set. What other implements of the kind she might have borne herself about with, one can only, even now, wonder at. Well, we are both, she and myself, bound—to this day—by the War Secrets Act. It scarcely matters, it appears, that Aunt Helen is ninety-four or better and that I was never, at any point in my career, since the impanelment I underwent in 1952—I ask your indulgence for my quite plainly having erred by a factor of two years when I earlier rehearsed for you the date I did—at, or in, Miami Retreat. It owes, or is owing, this small error, one must insist, to the "medication" that, disabling as its effects may sometimes seem to be, enables, or facilitates, or makes composable, the composition of these sentences. Listen, I could get killed for writing this. May it not be that I will be killed for writing this. It is not, for that matter, inconceivable that certain persons in the "publishing biz" might make themselves the instrument of my disassembly. Does one know? Can one know? One does not know. One cannot know. I went in—in 1952—as a Deutsch against "the Lishes." I did not "go in" as a citizen against whomsoever—as Helen had, as Adele, until her death, did. I complain not. I submit no complaint. It has been a great adventure. It has been one thrill after another. What a happiness, my stint! One cannot claim too lavishly for its part. May God keep this language safe! I, Gordon—Gordon!—speak, shriek, from White Plains as a patriot!

# ATTICUS
# AUGUSTUS LISH
# 1971 – 1986

---

COULD YOU USE A JOKE?

How about a joke?

Here's a joke.

There's somebody walking along and walking along which comes up to this other person which is walking along and the one of them says to the other one of them hey, how do, how's tricks, how's it going, how's every little thing, and so on and so forth, whereupon the other one of them says to the first one of them well, I lost my mother, you know, I had this very bad thing where I lost my mother, you know, there was this terrible thing where she was sipping a sip of water and the woman choked.

So the one person says choked, choked, that's too bad, choked, such a nice person, such a terrific person, just for her to choke—but so tell me, says the one person, so how is your father?

My father, says the other person, you want to know how's my father, says the other person—well, says the other person, the man keeled over, the man just stood there and keeled over—you

157

know, he was one minute just standing there like just like a nor-mal human being and then the next minute skip it, the next minute forget it, the man is out like a light, the man is down for the count, the man is as dead as a doornail, go get the shovels, that's it and that's it.

No kidding, says the person, that's too bad, says the person, what a shame, says the person, dead as a doornail, out like a light, down for the count, the man is a goner. But so tell me, says the person, so how is your wife?

My wife, says the other person, you are asking me how is my wife, so this is what you ask?

Sure, says the person, so how is your wife?

Well, says the other person, let's just say she got herself smacked flat by a bus—finished, curtains, forget it, kaput.

Oh boy oh boy, says the person, this one and that one, fin-ished, kaput—thank goodness you got children and you got grandchildren and you got probably got great-grandchildren and got nieces and nephews and so forth and so on for them to come to you in your loneliness and for them to come to you in your misery and for them to come to you in your grief so as for them to look after you and for them to console you and for them to give you like, you know, like comfort and things.

Oh, them, says the other person, all of them, says the other person—the other person says look, says listen, says you'll laugh, don't laugh, but them too, all of them too, they are all of them, every one of them, dead.

So what do you think?

Was it a scream or was it a scream?

Because this was the joke.

Okay, maybe you didn't get it yet.

It's maybe too deep for you to get it yet.

Look, it's not for everybody, you know?

Nobody ever said everything was going to be for everybody, you know?

For God's sake, it's a joke that says something, you know?

It's a joke which makes a kind of statement about things, you know?

Didn't you ever stop to think there's jokes and there's jokes— but what about the kind of a joke which makes a kind of statement about things which is deep?

All right, all right—how about this one about this person— Lish, Lish!—and he is going along and going along, whereupon he, you know, he meets this other person—and so like the person Not Lish, this person Not Lish says to Lish, he says to Lish, he says, "Hey, so how's it going? So what's up? So how's, you know, so how is like, you know, every little thing?"

To which Lish says, "Oh, you know."

"No," says Not Lish. "Not actually," says Not Lish. "I don't unless you tell me," says Not Lish.

"Well," says Lish. "You want specifics?" says Lish. "You want the actual specifics of what times what is up for me, Lish?"

"Right," says Not Lish. "The kidlinks," says Not Lish. Says Not Lish, "The boys and the girls, the sons and the daughters, the offspring, the issue, the issuance."

"Got a better one for you," says Lish. "Tell you what," says Lish. "There's this better for you," says Lish. "Let's just us go ahead and try this other one," says Lish. "Don't you want for me to tell you this other one?" says Lish. "Look," says Lish, "you be my brother and I'll be Lish—like you be my long-lost brother and I'll be Lish and so like you come up to me, you just come along and come up to me and you say to me hey, long time no see! And then I'll say to you you bastard you, you good-for-nothing bastard you, you got a lot of nerve just coming up to me and saying to me hey, long time no see to me after all of these years. And you'll say oh come on, come on, we're brothers, aren't we brothers? Don't we have like brothers like the same blood in our veins? Listen, what happened with us years and years ago, what happened between us years and years ago, what is it? Because it's ancient history. Because it's water under the bridge. Listen, you'll say to me, you'll say forgive and forget to me. You'll say to me it'll do you a world of good for you to just forgive and forget to me. You'll say to me you'll feel like a million bucks if you just say you'll forgive and forget to me. You'll say to me hey, come on, let's bury the hatchet, we'll bury the hatchet, let's kiss and make up, we'll kiss and make up, so what do you say, you'll say to me, are you ready for us like brothers to kiss and make up?

"And I'll say to you well, all right, all right, you're right, you're right. I'll say to you what good is it, a grievance, what good is it, a grudge? I'll say to you lucky for us, it's a lucky thing for us we just ran into each other like this after all of these years like this and after all of this heartache like this and after all of this loneliness like this and after so much misery and, you know, sorrow. Look, I'll say to you, hey look, I'll say to you, why don't you come on over to my place first thing tomorrow and what we'll do is we'll sit ourselves down and we'll sit there and have a cup of coffee together and, you know, we'll sit around and get together all over again like brother to brother together, peas in a pod?

"And you'll say to me hey, oh boy, I can't wait until tomorrow, I'm so happy about tomorrow, what a wonderful thing about tomorrow, tomorrow is the day of happiness and love.

"And I'll say to you so swell, so wonderful, so I will see you tomorrow, so don't forget about tomorrow, I am counting the minutes and hours until tomorrow.

"And you'll say to me terrific, terrific, tomorrow, tomorrow, you'll say to me don't worry, don't worry, am I forgetting tomorrow, who's forgetting tomorrow, I am not forgetting tomorrow, tomorrow is the day of loving brothers from one brother to another brother with love.

"And I'll say to you so okay, so here is a nice big hug and a nice big kiss for you until I see you tomorrow.

"And you'll say to me what a wonderful thing, a hug and a kiss from you, I couldn't be more excited, such a nice big hug and a kiss from you—except, you'll say to me, except wait a sec, you'll say to me, except wait a sec, you will say to me, except, you will say to me, could you please just brother to brother just wait a sec, you will say to me. And then you will say to me because hey, hey, you wouldn't, would you, maybe possibly have in the meanwhile like an extra kidney you could possibly lend me, would you?"

Okay, so you get it?

So compared with the other one, what do you think?

Better than the other one or not better than the other one?

If you had to choose?

If they made you choose?

If you had no choice except for you to choose?

If they came at you and they put a gun to your head and they said to you, you know, choose?

Hey, it wasn't, was it, that—oh boy—that this one was too deep for you too, was it?

Okay, so they're funny and deep.

For those which like them funny and deep, fine, fine—so here is another one which is funny and deep for you—which is where there is this person which is being buried and they are asking for everybody to stand there and say something about the person being buried and so there is this one person who says, there is this one person at the grave who says, there is this one person who when he has to speaks up and say something speaks up and says well, you know, his brother was worse.

Or the one even better than that one is the one where there is this person which meets this other person and the one person says to the other person so's how your brother and the other person says well, you know, it's terrible to have to say this to you but my brother passed away, my brother's dead, but so the first person says so how is your brother, is your brother in good health, and the other person says health, health, what are you talking about, health, I just told you, the man passed away, the man is no anymore, the man is dog food, the man is crowbait, the man is bupkis, but so the first person says so about your brother, how's he feeling, your brother, is your brother feeling all right, is your brother in what we call in the pink, is your brother in what we call good health, is your brother enjoying a nice healthy life, and the other person says listen, listen, didn't I just tell you, didn't I just this instant just stand here and tell just you, how many times does a person have to tell you my brother is finished, my brother is all gone, my brother is all over with, but so the first person says sure you told me, of course you told me, how could I not hear you tell me when you told me, but all I keep asking for is, I'm sorry, I'm sorry, but I just get such a kick out of it, I keep getting such a kick out of it when I hear the answer is when I ask, excuse me, excuse me, is the man is dead.

You like those?

So yes or no, you were or weren't pretty crazy about all of those?

Anyway, that's it for the jokes.

There aren't anymore jokes anymore.

There is nothing funny or deep or jokey anymore.

The rest, what's left—all of it, all of it!—it's all of it just surface and sad.

# FOR

# RUPERT—WITH

# NO PROMISES

———————

I DON'T THINK I would be writing this story if the facts did not force it. Actually, it's publishing this story that I do not think I would be doing unless I had a very pressing—really an irresistible—reason. It is probably necessary to say that I always imagined such a reason would one day come along. But I imagine many things—and why this one has caught up with me and most of the others have not is only the way it is with luck.

Not too much should be made of it, I suppose. My brother's, actually—*his* bad luck. But I believe that when I arrive at the end of what I want to say, I might also arrive at seeing the bad luck mine too. That's what comes of imagining things. It is also what comes of making promises you never intend to keep—or, worse, which you do not keep but which you try to convince somebody (even yourself) you have.

I made a promise like that once. It was a long time ago, and the one who inspired the promise was a child. A girl in this case. It was my conceit to think that she would remember what I had promised her, but I don't think she really did. After all, the year was 1944 and she must have had other things on her mind, there being a war going on at the time and her being twelve or thirteen or fourteen (despite a large opinion to the contrary, I am not all that much a student of children, and am especially inferior, I have often noticed, at pinpointing their ages), with all the calamitous worries that seize a child of such an age when its father has gone away. But she always wore a Campbell tartan and a watch much too big for her delicate wrist—and in those days in Devon and those days in my heart, a promise of any sort to a gentle child in plaid (with a weight too great for her arm) was not a thing I would not want to make. Besides, she had a little brother and always took good care of him, fretting if he was within earshot of a fact too awful for a small boy to hear.

At any rate, I promised her a story (I had wanted to be a writer then, and for too long a while thereafter I was one)—and some years later I wrote a story that was meant to appear to be the fulfillment of that promise.

Of course, it wasn't. A writer, especially the sort of writer I was trying to be, can't write stories like that—a pretty story when a child asks for one, a squalid story when *that* is the favor she asks. What I am paying for now is that I shabbily led her to believe otherwise. I wrote a story, a not very sincere story, nor a very graceful one (the years since demonstrate that the world disagrees with me in this judgment—but all I care about is that the story was mainly made up and is bruised by a very great fracture in its posture of narration), and when the piece was cast into print, I sent her a copy of the magazine sheets with a patch of paper pinned to the first page. I hadn't even the courtesy to set out my one sentence in my own hand, but instead typed the following, after a greeting that consisted of no more than the two lovely parts of her lovely English name: "I always keep a promise—I mean, p-r-o-m-i-s-e."

What I am paying for now is the lie I tried to get by with then.

I often read a Viennese logician who, I think, would go along with such reasoning. I think he would also go along with my reasoning that I am paying now for too much imagining. This is the kind of logic he favored when he lived.

It will presently be clear that I am, however, chiefly paying for my having a brother I love more than I love my silence. It will presently be clear that by publishing—and *only* by publishing—the little story I want to tell you, can I stop him from doing a thing he believes he must do. It is an act of extreme gravity, of extremest gravity, in all the spheres of spiritual prospect human imagining can consider. Or it is an act of no consequence at all. I am not certain. I am too overcome to rest for very long with a certain opinion. So I choose instead to do the safe thing—to put this story out for print.

All of this, I sincerely *promise*, will presently be very clear. One does not talk about what I am going to talk about, *and* talk in defiance of habit, unless one is utterly sworn to being very, very clear. I have sworn myself to the effort to let nothing interfere with clarity of the first order. Not even the sound of one hand clapping must be let to raise a noise along the straight planes of the sentences I am going to set down—but, reader, reader, how I hear that one hand clapping now!

My brother was an actor until radio gave out. After that, he tended bar on Fifty-fifth Street and on Fifty-seventh Street, and then he went to Oslo and then he went to Zurich, and when he came home he came home with a wife, a Swiss, a psychiatrist, and in time she proved herself a psychopath. But the time was not soon enough, for by then my beautiful brother and my handsome sister-in-law had a son. They named him, I felt honored to learn, David, called him Chap, and that is what he is called to this day, seventeen years later, fifteen of which Chap and my brother have not, not once, seen one another.

There was a divorce when Chap was two, and his mother, not long after, set up practice in El Paso, reasoning aloud that Chap's asthma would be more manageable there—the aridity—reasoning to herself, my brother supposes, that my brother would be taught what grief feels like.

You have my word for it that my brother did not need the lesson.

You have my word for it that he did everything short of seizing the office of the mayor of El Paso to force his residence in that town, close to Chap, close to the largest love in him.

You also have my word for it that my handsome sister-in-law did everything short of hiring ruffians to strong-arm the father well beyond the city limits. It was easy, considering. The woman, you will remember, is a psychiatrist, and a kind of despot therefore. And my brother, as you by and by will see as the facts are disclosed, was vulnerable in a very particular regard.

My brother—I shall call him by a different name here—my brother Smithy would return to New York with a sick heart, and when its sickening had worsened, he would go back to El Paso to cry out at the gates of the city. My mother tells us that these weekly, then monthly, pilgrimages went on for almost four years and were then gradually abandoned as the facts proved unmoving, unalterable, permanent. I was living in New England then, kept in very random touch with family, and—it will be no surprise to them if I admit it—discouraged them from doing other than returning the discourtesy. You see, at that time I was still dominated by the pretension of writing, although I was well past the point where I had fled from doing it in public. But, of course, I did hear from my mother and from my sister—and when Smithy had moved back to New York from Switzerland, from Smithy himself—that he had taken a second wife, a Swiss again, a woman somewhat older than the first and anything but a psychiatrist. This sister-in-law, whom I have not seen to this day, had banking as her profession, and still has it.

I do not need to see her to know that she is handsomer than the psychiatrist, for her photographs show up in the magazines and in a newspaper that is regularly attentive to very handsome and very active women, and my mother clips and forwards every single picture through an agent who has long given excellent service as an intermediary. And Smithy, who telephones often now that I have devised a truly private line, never fails to remind me that I am the brother-in-law of one of the world's most admired women.

But I do not need Smithy's reminding, nor my mother's clippings, to know how breathtaking Margaret must be—for the child of her marriage to my brother I have five times seen in the flesh, and he is the very word of loveliness, in this as in all things.

The boy's name is Rupert—and he is the child of all our dreaming.

If I say more about Rupert in regard of his unearthliness, I will not be for long free from confusion. I will—what I want to tell you will—fall victim to the disorder of sentiment, and I have promised you clarity. I have also promised someone squalor. I now intend, with reverence and with haste, to keep both promises— and to save my brother, and everyone else, in the bargain.

Rupert will be five on his next birthday. This is the last I will say about my brother's second golden son, comma purposely omitted. The next voice you hear will be Smithy's, and I can make no boundaries for *him*. *His* italics are entirely his own.

"Stoke up a cigarette; this is going to take a long time."

"I quit smoking. Snuffed my last butt the tenth of October. If Mom would tell you *anything*, she'd tell you *that*, and you promised me you were going to start *listening* to Mom, remember?"

There was a silence—not a good silence.

"Smithy? Hey, buddy, you there?"

"Please don't buddy me right now, Buddy. Please. And *please* don't kid around. I've finally thought the thing out, and what I've got to do—Buddy, dear God, I cannot believe I am saying this out loud—I am going to kill my son."

I did not shift the receiver to my other ear. I did not do anything that I can especially remember. I think if I had had a cigarette handy, I would have lit it. If there had been cigarettes in this house, I would have smoked them all. If I could have asked him to wait a half hour, I would have gone into town and bought a carton. Anyway, I did nothing—and I *said* nothing—because it was progressively occurring to me that I did not know *which* son Smithy meant, and that maybe *he* did not know either, and that if I said something that suggested one boy or the other, the suggestion might tilt my brother in one direction or the other.

Have I told you that my brother has twice *been away*? I know I haven't—because that is a fact that would certainly mislead you, and the one thing this piece of writing must *not* do is mislead you. But when one has a brother who has *twice* been away and who *married* a psychiatrist, one can oneself be misled by such facts. You cannot read enough of the Viennese logician to escape *certain* facts, and these may be among them.

"Buddy? Buddy, did you hear what I *said*? You want to go get a smoke now, big brother?"

And then he started crying, sobbing wretchedly. I had always imagined men could cry like this, but I had never heard it. It went on for a long time, and I was glad it did, because I believed that whatever had given it to occur would wear itself out this way and that would be that.

But it wasn't. Smithy stopped his weeping as abruptly as he'd started it, and when he began his first new sentence, it moved to its period with austere dispassion.

There's something else I have not told you. If he wanted, my brother could give the Viennese logician cards and spades. Smithy is very, very smart, endowed with an intelligence unsurpassed in our family and as statuesque as any I've come across. Moreover—and this is why I am not sure I am doing the right thing but only what I, like our Smithy, am convinced I must do—Smithy's unyielding custom is rationalism, all the way to the gallows if this were his destiny. There has never been anyone who could break him of the habit, and this goes for our older brother too—who could, just mentionably, break anyone of anything if he wanted to, and who would not flinch over breaking himself into nineteen pieces to do it. Except Smithy of his rationalism, of course.

But our big brother never had a very long run at it.

Anyway, Smithy's next sentence, and all the sentences that rolled along after that one and that I would not have dared to interrupt even to assert *Fallacy of the Middle!* were proportioned and stately in the organization of their argument. And this is what my brother said—and why my brother has concluded that he must kill his son—and why I am publishing what the reader may apprehend as a "story," but which Smithy, ever the rationalist, will understand as a disclosure one step short of my informing the police and a step quite far enough to stop him in his tracks.

And, of course, the boy Chap will have his fair warning.

It is the least a loving uncle who has made his fortune (and his misfortune) writing can do. He can write as he is able. He can write a "story" that no one but the ones who most matter to him will quite be certain is true. I *do* see now that it is only through the miracle of the falsehood of fiction that I can catch up the people I love from the truth and consequences of what they might do. The cost to me is very slight in comparison—the exception in a habit for silence (Are you smiling now, dear dead brother, master of ceremonies in all my deliberations?) and the reinstatement, for a time, of the shame that covers me whenever I play the thief of hearts and come like a highwayman to the unsuspecting page.

*Speak*, Smithy! I am the instrument by which you may submit your supreme reasoning—and the dark circumstance that stirred it to unfold its awful syllogism. And when you have stated your case, I will return for a parting courtesy to the reader, a gesture I swear to be greater than that to which I proved equal when I wished to say the right thing to soothe that splendid girl of Devon. I am thinking I owe a very particular politeness to the reader—who, for the purpose before us, and as do his mother and father, I call Chap.

*Listen*, Chap. The father of your body is speaking to you. Will you recognize his voice? You were not much more than two years old when you last heard the peculiar American resonance that made your dad a regular on *Rosemary of Hilltop House* and *When a Girl Marries*, a kind of choked vibrancy that must have softened when he blessed you to sleep and drew the covers up to just under you chin, high enough that not one whisper of cold would chill your breast, but not so high that your restlessness would slip the blanket higher and impede the glorious song of your breath. This is the father of your body whose voice you are going to hear. Will it be at all familiar to you after fifteen voiceless years? Will it frighten you to hear a silence broken? Certainly the speech he makes will seem frightening—for it is a statement in support of his decision to secure your death. But it is, nonetheless, a reasoned argument, and if you are your father's son, Chap, you will see he has a point.

*Listen*, boy! A brother I love like life itself, your true father, on the fourth day of November, by long-distance telephone, just after the dinner hour, his voice all repose, his heart deranged, in tumult, said *this*:

"I have a pad and pencil here, and it's all worked out, that thing you know I do with columns, this on one side, that on the other. Buddy, can you grab a piece of paper and something to write with? I think it'll help—I think it'll help if you make notes as I go along. I mean, it's just that I want you to know how it happened. Most of it has been happening for years. I think it has always been in the back of my mind since Pert was born. Maybe even before that, in a crazy kind of way. Maybe it dates back to when I kissed Chap goodbye and could never get back to kiss him again. In any case, I don't want you to think this *wasn't* among the premonitions that always go on in my head—because the head will *do* these things, Buddy, and you just can't, you know, stop it. Aren't you the expert in that subject? I'm rambling; I'm sorry. All right, I'm going to pick it up from what I've got *written* here. By the numbers, okay, big brother?

"About two weeks ago—hell, I know the *exact* day, who am I kidding?—Scharfstein told me I've got it bad. Wall-to-wall cigars and three packs of Raleighs a day for almost twenty-five years, and I get cancer of the goddamn *spleen*. I've always agreed with you that Scharfstein is a bastard, but his medicine is the best. Anyway, he sent me over to Sloan-Kettering that afternoon, and by the next morning they'd confirmed. Three to six months with routine measures, maybe another three to six with heavy anti-protein therapy. But that's it—that's tops.

"Maggie knows, of course. I didn't tell Mom or any of the rest, although I promise I will just as soon as I can figure out how I want to do it. And maybe you *can* help me with *that*. For the time being, all I'm doing is getting my life in order, squaring away my affairs, as Maggie would call them. Everything's pretty shipshape, actually—all the durables. There's plenty of money and there's nobody better than Maggie at managing. Then there's *Pert*—and that's, of course, clear sailing too. He could be the President of the United goddamn *States*, or change the theory of zero, and *this* won't stop him. My being dead, I mean— my dying. Pert could *be* anything, *do* anything. You know him; you've seen the probability for yourself. You just have to take one look at him to *know*.

"Except there's this one thing—and that's Chap. And if you don't mind, Buddy, I think I want to refer to Chap as David from here on out. There's David—*he's* the one thing. There's my son and there's my son—and *that's* the mathematics of it for you there! Are you following me? Because you better be doing it.

"What David's mother has done lots of divorced women do—I know that. Except I think she's done it better. But I'm only guessing, of course—because for fifteen years the evidence has been withheld from me. Can you believe it, Buddy? With people who feel about blood the way we do? Not one word, not one touch, in fifteen *years*? Jesus God, the woman is a trained *analyst*. If she can unravel a synthesis, I guess she can ravel a good enough one up. Can you just imagine what she's probably *achieved* with that boy? It's not just a job of contamination we're talking about—it must be more like the making of a biological system refined to a single aim. Of course, I'm only guessing—but that's where my imagination takes my reasoning—and what else do I have to go on?

"I *believe* in David's rage. Let's just say it's an article of faith with me—and with me dead, that rage will logically get pinned on *Pert*, don't you see? Loathing, envy, spite, you name it—and all of it susceptible to even greater intensity when David actually finds out what Pert *is*. I mean, what I see happening, when I'm gone, when all the rest of us are gone, Margaret and you and Mom and me and that woman—Buddy, I just *can't* say her name, not even now—I see a world with just the *two* of them in it— an openness named Rupert, who owns all my heart, and a man named David with a heart with so much hate in it. What would Rupert ever know of what his brother must feel for him? How could Rupert ever *imagine*? No boy could—no boy like

Rupert—and, Buddy, you know what Rupert is like. He is all light—a lightness, this one luminosity.

"Pert would never *guess* even. But I can. *More* than that—I *know*. David will wait, he will wait his time—like his mother, he will be a creature of stark determination, patient, deliberate, a fury waiting for his chance. All right, perhaps I'm imagining *too* much. Perhaps it will never come to that—something violent, an injury, a killing, who knows? Perhaps instead it will be a civilian act, but decisive, devastating—David sitting on some committee that Rupert happens to be petitioning, David behind the interviewer's desk for some job Rupert must have, David installed at a judicial bench before which Rupert pleads his case, David standing with gloved hands while Rupert lies beneath him, chest swabbed and bare to the scalpel—hell, I don't know, Buddy, but I know it'll be *something*. Some way none of us can predict, my firstborn will stalk my second, find a way to hurt *him* because my death *robs* him of his chance to hurt *me*.

"Look, there's nothing fishy in this, but I don't want to talk anymore—and besides, I'm calling from home and, with Maggie in the house, it's making me jittery—and I right now can't chance being *jittery*. I'll telephone tomorrow—around noon— so for Christ's sake, *be* there. Because I gave Scharfstein my promise I'd come in and see him in the morning—the jerk thinks he can teach me how to die—and I plan to fly up to Hanover in the afternoon. I guess Mom wrote you that David started Dartmouth this fall—all the way from Texas to my *brother's* backyard! Buddy, he writes these letters to his grandmother that I cannot believe and *do* not believe—like a *geometer's* made them. It gives me the willies to see them, but Mom always makes sure I do. He writes to *her*! Does he write to *me*? Does he answer *one* goddamn letter? Anyway, that's where he is and that's where I'm going tomorrow to get it taken care of. Jesus, man, I've got to *choose*, don't you see—and I choose *Rupert*!"

Your father hung up, Chap, with the delivery of that declaration. I didn't wait until the next day, though. I called him back right away—and this time I did get a piece of paper and a pencil—for no good reason, actually, but in moments of this kind one sometimes does things like this. I didn't say much. I didn't try to argue with him. I don't think I then knew what arguments to argue *with*—and I am not certain I know that even now. All I did know was that I had to try to stop him—not because there was in me a conviction that held him *wrong*—but only because there was a will in me to keep him from doing what he said. He did not answer right away, but when he did lift the receiver I immediately said, "Me again," and then I heard him say, "Mags, I've got a call and I need to talk in private. I'm sorry, but I need to," and then there was a moment's quiet and then my brother said, "Yes?" and I knew there was no arguing, nothing to do but state the livable range marked off by the mad logic of his assumptions.

"I have one thing to say," I said, "and that's this. Let it rest for three months. They've guaranteed you three months, at *least* three months, so you can wait that long and *then* do it. Not saying you *shouldn't* do it—just saying you can wait the three lousy months. Not that I think you'll change your mind—or that I'm sitting here trying to get you to—but just that you're in this position where you *can* add three months to Chap's life with no danger to Rupert. The minimum they've given you is the minimum you *can* and therefore *must* give Chap."

I was writing the numeral 3 again and again across the paper that I had pressed with the heel of my hand up against the wall. But the plaster was making them come out crooked, no matter how carefully I tried to control the pencil.

Chap, your father said, "Yes," and then he hung up the phone. He hung up without one other word. But the word he had uttered left no doubt—it was said so I would know there was no doubt. My brother knew that I knew he would do it—that your father would give you all the life he could.

That was the fourth of November.

I began writing these sentences that night, *last* night—and as I write this sentence now, it is morning.

I promised a courtesy, and this is it. I make this gesture to exist in the place of all the gestures I have not made. I am keeping every promise I have not kept. I am leading along to this courtesy everyone I have loved and ever misled.

There is an American writer, a woman, the only American writer I read. She has not written many stories, so it is no great undertaking to read everything she has written, which she has let have a life in print, that is. I take it that her public, unlike mine, is very, very small. This, I believe, is because she is unwilling to mislead, as I have so very often done and then tried to undo by my silence and now am trying still harder to undo by this last speaking up.

It *is* a great undertaking to understand even *one* of her stories, such as the one she brought forth into the world about two years ago. It is a story that begins as a story that this writer has stolen from another writer—but only because *he* had earlier stolen it from *her*. It was *her* story, she says, and it has to do with magic and with miracles and with many, many things. I think it had to do with everything.

Near to its infernal conclusion, the story happens on the writings of a very wise man, a man now in prison for knowing too much—about the weakness of man and about the terrible power of God, never more terrible than in the performing of His justice.

Among these writings, as the story calls the wise man's diaries, there is a tale the criminal has recorded.

Here is the tale.

A father is in a concentration camp. He learns that the list for the next day's gassings includes the name of his son, a boy of, say, twelve. So the father bribes a German (a diamond ring, he promises) to take some other boy instead—for who will really know *which* boy is taken? But then the father is uncertain of the rightness of his design. So he goes for guidance to the rabbi in the camp. And the rabbi will not help him. The rabbi says, "Why come to me? You made your decision already." And the father says, "But they'll put *another* boy in my son's place." The rabbi hears this, and he says, "Instead of Isaac, Abraham put a ram. And that was for God. Whereas you put another child, and for what? To trick the devil."

The father says, "What is the law on this?"

The rabbi answers, "The law is don't kill."

The next day the father does not deliver the promised bribe, and the Germans kill his son.

The father wanted a miracle, and he decided God would not give it.

But God did.

God created a father who could abide with the facts.

Oh, Chap, silent son, and all the beloveds I have promised, dear brother in heaven and dear brother still on earth, *this* is the one mir—I mean, m-i-r-a-c-l-e—there is. And you, Rupert, melodious child of our dreaming, for your birthday I give you this gift. It is the lesson I have placed before you—for when you are five and must be strong enough for the five fine candles aflame on your cake.

*Breathe.*

Now blow them all out.

Now good luck and long life.

# AFTER

# THE BEANSTALK

---

T HE ONE LOVE of my life was Beatrice, a dog of some kind.
As for her sentiments, it convincingly appeared Beatrice
more than amply reflected the experience of my emotion.
Goodness knows that whatever modest attention I might let be
sent in her direction the thing would answer with such a frenzy
of delight one feared the exertion might do the creature in. But
Beatrice lived and lived, and must have come to quite a great age
actually, considering that it was promptly on the accomplishment
of my birth that she had been made over to me as a gift, this by
Aunt Enid and Uncle Jack, in an earlier century. I had always understood dogs to suffer—in arithmetic terms, of course—a more
severe constraint within the natural precinct. It would have oc-
curred to me, in this regard, for example, that I should prove to
outlive Beatrice by a rather notable margin, all things being
equal. But truly, truly, I ask you, when are they ever? For there I
was, just managing to limp gingerly into the impressive decrepi-
tude of a very latterly decade, yet there also was Beatrice, doubtless more ancient than myself—the arithmetic concerning this

computation will not be at all taxing for even the most deficient reader—still continuing to conduct herself in the old manner. By what means, by what means, I put it to you, had my companion succeeded in eluding the penalty of the years? But just look at her, persisting with every vigor at the acquitting of those chores whose number Beatrice had obtained from Aunt Enid at the time of this person's having taken her final leave of us. I mean to say, it still happened that I had only to glance up from by studies at any time of night or day to espy this good and earnest beast toiling away with the fiercest of energies as she sought the completions and perfections of the dwelling we had for so long an era shared one with the other. To be sure, it would have been quite inconceivable to me that I should have permitted myself to slip into the last sleep without wondering aloud at the marvel Beatrice, in the mutt's mere being, revealed to me. And so it was that I, Gordon—Gordon!—touched Beatrice ever so lightly (it had become a rather unpleasant procedure for me to do much other than to read) upon the shoulder whilst this mysterious animal was making all speed past me in pursuit of errands with whisk-broom and dustpan.

"Dear dog," I said, "one sees you absorbed in labors for the common good, so please to forgive me for this interference and, too, for the impertinence which occasions it, but I should like to inquire of the heavens how can it be that every evidence of life keeps flourishing in yourself even as in me so slight a display of it endures."

Beatrice said, "Seeing that you ask, the answer is this—I am not what you see."

"Not what I see?" I said, too stunned to be quite compre-
hending of the event now in motion before me. "What, then, if
not what I see?" I said, still construing myself as a figure adream.

"A princess, but of course," Beatrice replied, conveying in
her style of speech a certain impatience with my amazement.

"Then a piece of magic has been worked upon you and you
are, as a consequence," I exclaimed, quite beside myself with the
triumph of my surmise, "an enchanted dog!"

"Right!" Beatrice confirmed. "A curse, a spell, a charm—
you name it."

"Was it," I asked, and none too bravely, I will admit, "Aunt
Enid who did it to you?"

"No, no," Beatrice sighed," letting fall both dustpan and
whiskbroom in a show, I concluded, of no small annoyance with
me, "not her, but him—that fucker Jack, the motherfucker."

"Please, Beatrice, please!" I erupted, ashamed for the both of
us at the intemperance of her diction. "I must beg you to realize
I had not known to this very time that you could talk, nor either
that you are, in truth, one transformed—and most assuredly not
a household hound, it must be assumed, but a rather handsome
woman, I expect the case must be, one who would very likely
seek to amuse me in a fashion quite beyond my power to imagine—and of noble bearing, you say, of nothing less than noble
bearing!"

At this, Beatrice retrieved her implements and settled a none
too forgiving gaze upon me. "Look," she said at length, "my
father was a monarch, yes, and me, I am some terrific piece of

ass, depend upon it—which, conjecture that it is, is nevertheless probably how come your weird relation had to hex me—the stinking dirty creep!"

It was then that I spoke to my pet thusly: "Oh, oh, Beatrice, I beg you, I beg you, no more of this coarseness—it is altogether too distressing to me for me to hear it from your lips, not least when I now have such a deal of everything to struggle with within myself to make an adjustment to if we are, you and I, to produce a future for ourselves from this present—that you can converse, to cite the first of these items, that you are prospectively a most sumptuous instance of womanhood, to cite the second of these, that you promise incalculable erotic bliss, to cite the third, and that you must certainly be rich as well as royal, to cite now a fourth and a fifth."

"Kiss me, Gordo!" Beatrice commanded, flinging aside the symbols of her servitude and thrusting her open body at me. "Kiss me, pal, and all—big bucks, fabulous pussy, even life everlasting—shall be yours!"

"Sounds pretty swell to me," I acknowledged. But, collecting myself not a jot too soon, I drew myself safely apart and issued the ensuing statement: "I absolutely refuse, precious thing, to surrender myself to the conditions—and therefore to the destiny—of any joke that I, Gordon—Gordon!—have not myself invented, just as I would also refuse, please be aware, to forego even one of the several myselves deployed in the foregoing utterance."

The brute's eyes widened.

One noted, I note—with a twinge of unseemly satisfaction perhaps—that it was no longer my turn to be the party taken aback. Yet my heart was swift to soften at the spectacle of melancholy that I had, in my recall to form, inspired—and, accordingly, awful as it was for me in my ruined substance to do, I reached out my fingertips and caused them to create a sort of consoling effect upon the nearer of the cur's ears.

"There, there," I crooned, "thrilling as it would be—I don't deny it for an instant—to inaugurate your freedom to yourself, on the whole, sweetness, I think that I should much prefer the fame of my having had a talking dog."

Well, I needn't report the bitch bit me good and proper at that. Nor that I do not expect the wound she gave me—good God, the offense of one's biology, the incommensurable insult of it!—ever to give itself to mending.

That's it.

It needs only to say no regrets. It's been the first and last of my amours—witty, just, and fatal.

# HOW THE
# HEAD COMES OFF

---

ALL RIGHT, we each have seven cards. Seven cards have been dealt to you, seven cards have been dealt to me. Let us say that, between the two of us, it is I who had done the dealing, yes? All right—if it is I who has been the one to deal, then you play first.

Yes, yes, yes, of course—but what do you play?

Let us say that you play the seven of diamonds.

Very good, you have played the seven of diamonds.

All right, my options are these—play a seven, or play a diamond, or play an eight.

All right, why an eight?

Eights are wild. This is why an eight. It can always "be" an eight.

But do I have an eight?

No, I do not have an eight.

Moreover, if I had an eight, it would be smarter not to play the eight—no, no, no, not at this "stage" of the game.

I mean that when this "stage" of the game is the beginning "stage" of the game.

Ah, but what if I had three eights?

Or all four eights?

In other words, what if I had in my hand such an abundance of eights that it might not do ruinous harm to my long-term prospects for me to spend spendthriftly from my supply of eights?

But skip it.

I have no surplus of eights.

To be sure, I have in my hand not even one goddamn eight.

Ah—so what do I do?

Yes, yes, yes, what do I do?

Play a seven? Play a diamond? Yes, yes, yes, these are possible plays—a seven, a diamond—either of these are the possible plays, are they not? But one must have the one or have the other in one's hand, must one not?

I mean I must.

But I do not.

So now what, now what?

I'm sevenless and diamondless, not to mention eightless—so now what?

All right, the answer is I pick.

I may—or must—pick.

I can "go pick," taking from the "deck" cards in hopes of my coming upon a playable card.

Meaning, taking cards from the aggregate of cards not dealt when the cards were, you know, dealt.

In other words, that's the "deck," the undealt cards.

The thirty-eight cards.

Because, at this "stage" of the game, the "deck" is constituted of the result achieved when fourteen is taken away from fifty-two, given that neither of us has thus far been made to "go pick," correct?

Correct.

But now I, your opponent, must "go pick."

All right, I pick the jack of hearts.

No good.

I pick the deuce of clubs.

No good.

I pick the eight of spades.

Ah.

Ahhh.

An eight!

But do I use it?

No, no, no, eights are wild, or eights are "wild," but let their "wildness" be "preserved."

I pick again.

This will be my fourth pick.

How many picks is one allowed when one must "go pick"?

The answer is five.

The rule is this—when one "goes and picks," the pickable limit is five cards.

I pick.

I have picked.

The four of diamonds!

Thank God.

All right, I play the four of diamonds. The other cards that I have picked, the jack, the deuce, the eight, these all get stored, placed, preserved—in my hand, or in my "hand." Whereas I play, have played, can play the diamond "on" your diamond.

Good.

Your turn to play.

You search your "hand."

You see in it—rulingly—a diamond.

Yes, yes, but what if the set screw is stuck?

All right, let us suppose the set screw, so-called, is stuck, is "frozen," as they say—what then?

Or, "then what"?

Look at it this way—you arrive at the cemetery.

Everyone trudges, everyone traipses, everyone trundles inside—where there is a frosted window at which, it is plain, one applies. Or, let us say, goes to, stands at, stares into, and lightly agitates the bell that is there for you to summon the cemeterian inside.

Good.

"You are?" the fellow says.

One answers, "Lish, the child of, the husband of—what difference?"

Ah, but suppose the set screw had come undone.

Or that you had played the seven of spades.

Or that I had not been "dealer."

But it did not and you did not and I was.

# SOPHOCLES

———

TAKE EGG. Boil until hard-cooked. Crack shell. Hold under running water. Remove shell. Set shell aside. Peel away white. Set white aside. Use heel of spoon to mash yolk in mid-size mixing bowl. Add one teaspoon heavy cream, one tablespoon granulated sugar, one teaspoon confectioners' sugar, three teaspoons almond extract, dash salt. Blend until blended consistency has been achieved. Set mixture aside. Take half cup shortening, two cups sifted flour, one teaspoon salt, four tablespoons ice water. Blend with fork. Melt two sticks unsalted butter and fold in. Add two teaspoons vanilla extract. Shake in ground cinnamon and nutmeg to taste. Cover with dampened towel and set aside in warm, dry place. Core eight apples. Cream three bananas. Take one cup sour cream, half cup sweet cream, quarter cup molasses. Blend three tablespoons dark brown sugar with quarter cup unsalted butter. Add half teaspoon baking powder. Turn when bubbles appear. Set mixture aside. Heat bacon drippings, peanut oil, and corn oil in shallow frypan. Drain excess into brown paper bag. Pour remainder into buttered casserole. Sprinkle with paprika. Pat dry. Remove from pan. Allow milk to "billow." Cut in four servings of finely chopped cabbage. Put seven egg yolks, two pints buttermilk into large mixing bowl. Beat until ingredients are thoroughly moistened. Cream butter while gradually adding sugar. Add egg mixture to hot milk in saucepan. Set aside and take two tablespoons strained orange juice and eight-ounce jar apricot preserves. Cut pecans coarsely. Pour and spoon into prepared pan. Add half cup condensed milk, half cup evaporated milk, whole cup skim milk. Cook until substance has clarified. Let cool before refrigerating. Then bring gently to boil. Stir in apples and "shave" top with well-chilled knife. Beat vigorously until thick. Set this aside. Crush four vanilla beans with curd mallet. Divide with scissors into one-inch pieces. Transfer mixture to baking tin. Core more apples. Fold in eggs. Fold in pecans. Beat until stiff. Where's your cooked egg white? Don't forget your cooked egg white! Cut shortening into safflower oil. Remove cabbage from double boiler. Steam and then spread until surface is crumbly. Beat with whisk. Set aside. To begin sauce, take one quart okra, two pints tomatoes, two chopped onions, salt and pepper to taste. Take off skin and slice thin. Shake until greens are engulfed. Combine and keep beating. Prepare greased sheet. Allow contents to regroup. Dice and remove grated walnuts. Mixture is "ready" when peaks appear. Set aside and boil without stirring. Is it brittle? Discard and start again if brittle. What happened to vanilla beans? Crush more vanilla beans. Take creamed bananas. Pat dry. Remove from bowl. Lift gently. Combine. Fold back towel. You dampened it, didn't you? Didn't you dampen it? You didn't, you didn't, you didn't dampen it! You took this for a joke and didn't dampen it, did you? See the brittleness? Weren't you warned? You were warned, weren't you?

Take egg.

No, forget it—don't take egg.

Go get eight pounds stewing meat.

Hack away gristle.

Hack away suet.

Rip out bone.

# I'M WIDE

MY WIFE AND SMALL SON were away for the week, having removed themselves from the day-to-day predicament for a brief travel to a place of better weather. I was fine the first night, and remained equally fine the second and third, feeding myself from the cabinets and cupboards and pantry and doing what seemed expectable in the way of tidying up. Yet each night I would put off my hour of retirement a trifle longer than that which had found me seeking the sanctuary of my bed the night previous—so that by the fourth night, it was virtually daybreak when I sought the security of blankets and pillow. Mind you, I was not passing the sleepless hours in any particular fashion, aside from the regularity of those few moments that saw to my nutrition and the succeeding clean-up of the premises. But I cannot tell you what precisely I was doing, save that I think I spent the greatest fraction of the time moving from room to room and regarding the objects that appointed them. At all events, it was during the course of the fifth night of their absence—of my wife and small son, I mean—that I was suddenly, in my meanderings, captured by the sense that I had happened to come upon the thought of my lifetime. It was while beholding the seat of a wainscot chair of the Jacobean period, and while losing myself in the patina my week-by-week waxing of its surface had achieved, that I thought, Why wax? I mean, it was such a clamor, this notion— *Why wax?* Why, indeed, wax anything ever again when one could instead coat a surface with—ahh—shellac!

I was positively beside myself with excitement, gripped by a delirium of a quality I am not competent to describe. I remember thinking, My God, just look at me, an ordinary fellow abandoned by wife and child, now exalted in his possession of a piece of the most exquisite invention. I was quick to consider the punishing labors of all those persons who, for years by the eras, had applied themselves to the rude practice of spreading on and then of rubbing and buffing, this when one layer of shellac could end such oafish industry forever.

I went first to the shelves that we used for the storage of all inflammables, took what I wanted in the way of a can and a brush, and then made haste for my closet, there taking up the two pairs of shoes I then owned and carrying them into the living room, stopping en route to gather several sections of the Sunday paper from the stack it is our habit to keep accumulating from Sunday to Sunday.

Oh, you goon! Did you honestly think it was the furniture I meant to have a go at? Great heavens, no. Shellac on wood has been done and done—whereas who'd ever thought of *shoes*?

I arranged things.

I laid out paper.

I pried off the lid of the can.

I inspected the brush for dust, for hairs.

Have I said that wife and son are endowed with hair of the finest filament? In any case, I went to work, and left my efforts to dry, sleeping more satisfactorily than it had been my fortune to do in years.

But when I returned from my office the following evening, both pairs of shoes were still wet—two nights thereafter (I was appalled), they were no drier. It was only then that I realized I had been wearing galoshes.

I went at them with a razor blade, the shoes, scraping. I scraped and then I tried a solvent. I admit it—this time I didn't bother myself with newspaper. I no longer liked the floor any better than I liked my shoes.

I won't make this last forever.

I murdered those shoes.

I hacked at them—I dug and delved and stabbed.

Towards dawn, I dumped them in the trash, and got out the vacuum cleaner to suck up the shreds of leather. But I could see where there was no repairing the floor by such measures. The solvent had eaten holes through the varnish. It was festered, that floor. It was an infestation.

I skipped my office after scrubbing off the stain on my hands. I went in galoshes straight to a shoe store, took a seat, stuck out a galosh, said, "Nine-and-a-half, E. Give me a brogue."

"You mean wingtip?" said the simp.

"That's it," I said. "E. I'm wide."

"In a jiffy," he said, and the purchase was made, the whole ugly affair accomplished in minutes.

I was fine. All the way home, I was fine. For the rest of the day I ate biscuits and tidied and waxed those shoes. It was not until the new shoes seemed as shiny as they would get that I left off and squatted there gazing at things, studying the chairs and the tables, all the surviving surfaces that gleamed. It was then that I was willing to reckon with the rest of what I had said to that fop of theirs when he had asked why in the world was it that I was wearing galoshes now that the streets were empty of snow.

Oh, listen to me listening to myself!

"Listen," I said, "I got this boy, God love him, he's seven, and all he wants to do is do for me. So what happens? So when I'm not looking, what happens? Listen," I said, now raising my voice for the whole shoe store to hear, "that kid, that wonderful kid, he takes shellac to every last one of my shoes to put a lasting shine on them!"

I even laughed when everybody laughed.

Do you understand what I am saying to you? I winked my goddamn head off—me, a man.

# PHILOSOPHICAL

# STATEMENTS

---

S HUN NEGATIVITY. Eschew negativity. Send down negativity. Turn a cold shoulder to negativity. Never know the name of negativity. Make yourself the assassin of negativity. Befriend negativity not. Let negativity not enter in. Keep negativity out. Go away from negativity. Take flight from negativity. Rid thy house of negativity. Be free of negativity. Tear up the taproot of negativity. Throw off the garment of negativity. Eat not of the nutriment of negativity. Worry negativity. Usher negativity away. Shut your door to negativity. Spurn negativity. Scorn it. Smite it. Never call out to the servants of negativity. Hate negativity. Not to summon negativity's jinn. Unlearn negativity. Do unto negativity as you would the unclean. Let not your mind be near to negativity. Keep your mentation denegativized. Murder negativity. Trample down negativity. Negativity is catastrophe's furrow. Let it be unraveled, that which negativity has raveled up. Strangle negativity. Stop up your ears against negativity. Be wary, here comes negativity. Negativity is the goiter, the nevus, the milk leg, the whites. Never negativity. Go without negativity. Be not the mount for negativity's assault. Negativity moves in with beetles in his reticule. Negativity vexes, exasperates, peeves, itches. Negativity spoils. Have you negated negativity? Push away negativity. Push negativity off. Defy negativity. Expose the agents of negativity. Fear negativity's errand, mission, putrid device. Negativity has a plan—steal it, thrash it. Negativity nurses its children—let the nipple invent a worm. Negativity's song has a long, pale throat—does your axe not see its course? Negativity asks to eat at your table. Negativity wants to be your supper. Negativity leans in when the coverlet you raise up. Negativity prepares your dream, imagines your existence. Negativity watches, waits, is in no hurry. Look to proportion. Invite proportion. Follow proportion. Snatch at the skirt of proportion. Entice proportion's eye. Bend to proportion's purpose, curve to her languorous wile. Let proportion sweep your floor. Lead proportion in, heap honey onto her plate. Oh, sweet proportion, come quiet this perfidious heart! Proportion goes without corsets. Whisper not against proportion. Repeal proportion's torturer. Where proportion is, mischief is not. Witness the grace of proportion. Proportion's impeachment struggles on club feet. Be the pretty child of proportion. Enact proportion's business. Good light is proportion's work. Open your lips for proportion's kiss. Here soars proportion, all else plummets. Let proportion be your consort, your shepherd, your bride. Marry proportion. Wed proportion. Lift proportion onto your back. Inscribe nothing if proportion be not your instrument. Vehemence lies twisted in the bedclothes, proportion slumbers in oblivious repose. Proportion is content. Proportion is wise. Proportion's husband is rich. Where proportion walks, the path is underfoot. Next to proportion stands prosperity in shoes. Proportion abides. Proportion fits. Proportion adds up. Proportion knows the score. Proportion is no dope. Proportion is not an imbecile. Proportion is a smart cookie. Seize opportunity. Grasp opportunity with both hands. Opportunity's departure is never not punctual. He who would chase opportunity must begin not a day late, not a minute late, is even now late. Opportunity does not masquerade as a loiterer. Opportunity is fugitive. Latch the gate when opportunity is inside. Opportunity's warder cannot rest. There goes opportunity. Opportunity shouts no one's name. Children, children, to suffice is enough. He who is sufficient is sufficiency's master. She shall have sufficiency come hem her white gown. No tailor a thimble lends to sufficiency's sturdy wife. Sufficiency lets down her hair to harmony's warrior. Come, darlings, for princes do dance at the well! The water is chaste. Dark is the apron of the stable boy not unbusy at his rounds. Be not lazy, be not known to rue. Heaven's bed is always made, its quilt mended and warm. Descend, harmony—they would the banquet begin! Where fame goes does villainy not hasten ahead? Be cautious, be not a father. Stay home, Young Albert! Edward's cat is fat, Mary's duck is lost! Be smart, go by the book. Be smart, go by the board. If the rat today, then not the martingale tomorrow? Curry the badger, fasten the saddle. Reap not the fruit of the windwillow tree if Lately's daughter you would have pretty your couch. Larder on Monday, goose for the sabbath. Toil behind the lee horse, feed before bed on soup. Merry is the fool, sorry struts his teacher. Sweetmeats, quoths the thief; needles and pins, weeps the bailiff. Dance with the seamstress, dead in a fortnight. See a blind cobbler, starve the fox, catch the hare, tie the dog, choose the maid, bind the owl, pick the wool, tame the yarn, lock the box, bother the ox, spin the top, buckle the shoe, cool the pie, render the fat, scald the milk, dip the cream, rack the butter, iron the collar, scold the stew, take the broth, turn the fire, thicken the sauce, tether the goat, ask the cow, the carp, the dove, the hasp, the pan, the pot, the cheese, the chair, the hinge, the rag, the spoon, the fork, the button, the thread, the cake, the stocking, the candle, the cough, the curd, the grave, the dish, the hen, the bucket, the hook, the stick, the yoke, the belt, the stone, the salt, the rope, the cloth, the rake, the sleeve, the paste.

Therefore Tarski.

If Tarski, then not then Kripke?

# THE LITTLE
# VALISE

———————

FIRST OF ALL, I'm sorry this story takes place in a subway because I know I have told some other stories that have also taken place in a subway but I am sorry because the subway is where the story really takes place and I do not think it is the kind of a story where you would want to fool around with the place where it took place just because it happened to have been the same place where you said some other stories did.

Second of all, I'm sorry it has to be such a quick story but this is another thing—the fact that the story was, in real life, quick, and the fact that I just do not think, I honestly don't—okay, here we go again, here is my thinking again—that it would be the right thing for me to do if I were to fool around with how long a story it actually was just because of people and of what they expect from you as far as how long and so forth.

Third of all, let's get going, okay?—because it's late and I'm knocked out and there is no reason for us to go overboard with this and I'd really like to get to bed.

I get on the subway at the place where I usually get on, which is Ninety-sixth. I only mention the number to you—come on, what good are numbers in stories, right?—only because this way you can see how stuck I am with how long the story has to be— since it goes from Ninety-sixth Street to Fifty-first Street, which is the distance I have to go to go from my place—the place where I live, this is—to the place where I work.

Isn't distance the same thing as time or something?

Anyway, what isn't?

When you really get right down to it, is there anything which isn't?

Which is the point about the nun.

You take one look at her—I couldn't miss doing it because, first of all, the nun is sitting almost right straight across from me and because, second of all, the nun has the most beautiful face which I have ever seen—you take one look at her and you cannot stop looking at her.

The nun.

But she will not look back at me.

She will not look at anybody that I can see.

The thing I notice after I notice how beautiful the face of the nun is is that the nun will not look at anybody that I can see.

What I can see is that the nun is looking more or less in front of the tips of her shoes, which are black, of course, and which are right straight out in front of her, of course.

Then at Eighty-sixth Street there is a woman which gets on and who is going at it like a regular beggar.

Begging.

I don't have to tell you.

It is a public occurrence.

Asking for money, for food, for anything.

The thing of it is that she gets herself, the beggar, set up right straight in front of the nun.

But the nun never looks up to see any of this.

The nun is instead just looking at the same place, which I have told you is the place which is more or less right in front of her shoes.

The nun's.

The nun is not looking at anything but at what she is looking at—except am I in any position to tell you if the nun is actually seeing anything of what she is looking at or isn't?

I'm not, am I?

Anyway, I figure the nun, if she gets off before I get off, I will see her probably at least maybe touch the arm of the woman begging or touch the wrist of the woman begging—maybe whisper to her a blessing, if this is what they do, whisper blessings to women begging, or whisper to the woman begging, "Come with me and I will see to it that you are fed and bathed and given comfort and so forth and so on—bed, blanket, you know, clean sheets to sleep inside of."

But she didn't.

Oh, she got off before I got off, all right. The nun got off at Fifty-ninth Street and never even put her hand out anywhere near the woman I have been mentioning at all.

Did I tell you she had a little valise with her and off she went, the nun?

Me, I go the rest of the way to Fifty-first and then get off.

It's my usual routine per usual—Ninety-sixth to Fifty-first.

Anyway, here's the story.

That I would have followed the nun anywhere if I think she would have let me—especially after the look I see she has on her which I saw on her on her face when she goes past me and then went out with her little valise.

It was what I would have to tell you was a peeved look, you know?

Made to stop being, for a little bit, where she was—it must have peeved the hell out of her—the nun.

God, to be there—to be anywhere—the way this nun I was just telling you about was.

Just once.

Or—better—forever.

# SOPHISTICATION

———————

THE MAN WHO STOOD, who stood on sidewalks, who stood facing streets, who stood with his back against store windows or against the walls of buildings, never asked for money, never begged, never put his hand out. But you knew that's what he was doing—asking, begging, even though he made no gesture in your direction, even though all he did was fix you with his eyes if you let him do it, and, as you passed, made that sound. It was *doobee doobee doobee*—or it was *dabba dabba dabba*. It was always the same, and the one or the other, but you never tarried long enough for you to hear if there were more.

He was wearing high-heeled shoes the first time I saw him. They were women's shoes, or they were women's backless high-heeled slippers. I don't remember which. Yes, I think they were bedroom slippers—pale blue, furred, little high-heeled slippers.

I saw him the first week I moved here. I always saw him after that—it did not matter what the weather was. He was there in every kind of weather, backed up against a wall or against a store window—*doobee doobee doobee* or *dabba dabba dabba*.

He worked my neighborhood.

He did what he did in my neighborhood.

I gave him a dime that first week. He took it. If he was not begging, then he was taking money. But I never gave him anything after the one time.

I was angry about giving him that dime. I felt it marked me as a sucker. I don't think I would have felt that had he not shown up again the next day, the next week, every day of every week after that.

Every time after that first time I always passed him by—*doobee doobee doobee* or *dabba dabba dabba*, oh so very softly—angry that the man was there, a witness to the fool I was.

That dime should have saved his life, gotten his back off public construction, sent him away to another neighborhood, changed his song.

But he's gone now. He hasn't shown up for weeks.

It's a relief. I feel better about living here now—but it's not on account of that dime, not on account of the shame that I gave it and shame that I never gave another one after giving it. It's terror his absence relieves me of. It's the worst fear I ever had.

It was when the snows came this winter that I got very afraid of the man.

I want you to know how, I want you to hear how, the man got me so afraid.

I'd gone to get my son home from a playmate's house after dark. It wasn't that many blocks there and that many back. But the snow was at its worst and there was no one on the streets, not all the way there and almost not all of the way back.

We were just a block from home, my boy and I, and the man was on that block, standing on the corner, his back to the wall of something. There was no way home without passing him. I got my boy tight by the hand and took him out into the street to do it.

The man just stood there—no gesture, no hand reached out. He didn't get me with his eyes because I wouldn't let him do it. But there was no not hearing *doobee doobee doobee* or *dabba dabba dabba*—just always a whisper, but a whisper really loud.

A car came skidding along the street. My boy and I were moving up it now and that car was moving down it, skidding, sort of careening, a reckless driver playing in the snow.

I have such a childish imagination.

I thought: He'll hit us, that driver. I thought: My son will be hurt. I thought: There will be no one to help me, no one but the man I always passed.

I saw myself kneeling over my son. I saw myself begging the man for him to help.

I heard him answering—*doobee doobee doobee*.

Or *dabba dabba dabba*.

Very softly.

But this can't happen now, can it?

The man, hasn't the man gone away?

# FIRST REAPPEARANCE OF THE PRODIGAL SON

---

THERE WAS NOTHING I could think of to say to the woman. It occurs to me to wonder, however, if there had been a reason for me to. It is entirely plausible that she expected no attention from me at all—and that she meant to affirm, in her absent gazing at the close of her tale, to want no further of my presence, let alone some exhibit of utterance in anxious display of my having reckoned with, and run to ground, the significance of what she had just conveyed to me, which anecdote—on the surface, at any rate—was not much to speak of, was it? Merely—namely!—that the boy had succeeded, with no particular talent required of him to do so, at calling her aside from her distractions—the clearing of the chargers from the great table, the gathering there from of the slops for the hounds—this to ask of her if it would induce in her any pleasure for her to see him in his costume.

"Costume?" she said.

"Oh, yes!" said the boy, trembling, veritably trembling, with exclamation.

"Your costume?" said the woman.

"Quite exactly that," said the boy. "For, you know, for the band," said the boy. "So would you?" the boy said.

"But of course," the woman said, touching one of the implements still to be taken from the befouled damask spread all about them—implements or damask, she did not say which.

The boy went from the hall and, after an interlude longer than, it had seemed to her, so claimed the woman, the period of this person's expulsion from her netherness, returned to it—got up not as he had been but now in the manner of him who would do what he could, as ably as he could, to carry off the bearing of a certain particle in the brass section of an organization of souls who would, while making music, march.

"See?" the boy said.

"I see," the woman said.

"You like it?" the boy said, braid and brocade a rhyme thereinafter, she alleged to me, to be forever annealed to the far bronze bulkhead of her mind.

"Yes indeedy," the woman said, for the first detecting, she believed, the wet performance of long tongues slapped back into place in the mouths they had unfurled from.

Then the chewing.

She heard the dreadful chewing.

"It's lovely," she said. "It's your uniform," she said. "For when, for if, the band in town, the town band, plays," she said. "Oh, yes, I love it," the woman said she had said.

"Good, good," the boy said. "I think I sort of knew it,

Mother. I sort of think I knew you would, Mother," the boy said, now striking a pose for the woman, now concocting himself into the posture of one who would never rest until his horn had imagined its last note.

"That's it?" I said.

"That's what?" she said.

"The thing you wanted to have me hear," I said.

"He had," she said, "a hat."

I said, "Well, yes—but billed or furred?"

To which inquiry no reply was made to me that I could ever have made out, so loud was the cry, it must have been, for—if not death, then please, please!—at least for silence.

Well, did you ever!

Because I, for one, never heard anything like it, silence.

# DE PROFUNDIS

---

WHICH IS YOU take coffee, you take milk, you take sugar, or you take sugar substitute, depending on which your preference is, depending whether it's for sugar or for sugar substitute. Me, I always go for the substitute.

Then you go take some ice to it, depending if you have a blender which can deal with ice in it.

So I'm blending.

I'm blending with the reconditioned blender we went ahead and had reconditioned before one thing leads to another and everything goes and gets itself so haywire and she, guess what, drops dead from it.

Brother, does it work!

I'm telling you, talk about when a thing works!

Producing, you might say, on low power a nice type of low-powered type of smooth-powered output—and then, when geared up to full power, giving out more of a more powerful type of full-powered output but meanwhile not being self-induced by itself into erupting into the type of wave motion which you know how it can get crazy on you to the point where the contents of the canister is all of a sudden climbing the walls of the canister, making a wreck of the kitchen counter, not to mention the rest of the kitchen, from like, you know, from coming all of the way up and out from like this—down there!—vortex.

It's not called a vortex?

Well, guess who just cleaned up the tiles up.

Bleached the grout lines even.

You know the tile boundaries around them made of grout?

Grout boundaries!

So finish the blending and pour out the blendation—and sorry, I'm sorry, but it's sensational, it's a sensation.

Down her in a gulp.

Down the whole deal in one whole gulp.

Turns out it's the best darn drink which I have ever drunk.

So here I am—a widower, the widower—standing at the sink, thinking all credit to them which did the reconditioning, credit to the heavens to the outfit which turned around and did the reconditioning—rewinding the little motor for it, regapping the synapses of the switches for it, getting the wiring—isn't there a magneto, a terminal, a resistor?—fucking just right for it.

# THE

# MERRY CHASE

---

Don't tell me. Do me a favor and let me guess. Be honest with me, tell the truth, don't make me laugh. Tell me, don't make me have to tell you, do I have to tell you that when you're hot you're hot, that when you're dead you're dead? Because you know what I know? I know you like I know myself, I know you like the back of my hand, I know you like a book, I know you inside out.

You know what?

I know you like you'll never know.

You think I don't know whereof I speak?

I know, I know.

I know the day will come, the day will dawn.

Didn't I tell you you never know? Because I guarantee it, no one will dance a jig, no one will do a dance, no one will cater to you so fast or wait on you hand and foot.

You think they could care less?

But I could never get enough of it, I could never get enough. Look at me, I could take a bite out of it, I could eat it up alive.

But you want to make a monkey out of me, don't you. You want me to talk myself blue in the face for you, beat my head against a brick wall for you, come running when you have the least little complaint. What am I, your slave? You couldn't be happy except over my dead body? You think I don't know where of I speak? I promise you, one day you will sing a different tune.

But in the interim, first things first.

Because it will not kill you for you to do without, tomorrow is another day, let me look at it, let me see it, there is no time like the present, let me kiss it and make it well.

Let me tell you something, everyone in the whole wide world should only have it half as good as you.

You know what this is? You want to know what this is? Because this is some deal, this is some setup, this is some joke. You could vomit from what a joke this is.

I want you to hear something, I want you to hear the unvarnished truth.

You know what you are? That's what you are!

You sit, I'll go—I already had enough to choke a horse.

Go ahead and talk my arm off. Talk me deaf, dumb, and blind. Nobody is asking, nobody is talking, nobody wants to know. In all decency, in all honesty, in all candor, in all modesty, you have some gall, some nerve, and I mean it in all sincerity. The crust on you, my God!

I am telling you, I am pleading with you, I am down to you on bended knee to you—just don't get cute with me, just don't make any excuses to me—because in broad daylight, in the dead of night, at the crack of dawn.

You think the whole world is going to do a dance around you? No one is going to do a dance around you. No one even knows you are alive.

Just who do you think you are, coming in here like a lord and lording it all over us all? Do you think you are a law unto yourself? I am going to give you some advice. Don't flatter yourself, act your age, share and share alike.

Ages ago, years ago, so long ago I couldn't begin to remember, past history, ancient history—you don't want to know, another age, another life, another theory altogether. Don't ask. Don't even begin to ask. Don't make me any promises. Don't tell me one thing and do another. Don't look at me like that. Look around yourself, for pity's sake. Don't you know that one hand washes the other?

Talk sense.

Take stock.

Give me some credit for intelligence. Show me I'm not wasting my breath with you. Don't make me sick. You are making me sick. Why are you doing this to me? Do you get pleasure from doing this to me? Don't think I don't know what you are trying to do to me. You think you're so smart.

Don't make me do your thinking for you.

Shame on you, be ashamed of yourself, have you absolutely no shame?

Why must I always have to tell you?

Why must I always drop everything and come running?

Does nothing ever occur to you?

Can't you see with your own two eyes?

You are your own worst enemy.

What's the sense of talking to you? I might as well talk to myself. Say something. Try to look like you've got a brain in your head. You think this is a picnic? This is no picnic. Don't stand on ceremony with me. The whole world is not going to step to your tune. I warn you—wake up before it's too late.

You know what?

A little birdie just told me.

You know what? You have got a lot to learn.

I can't hear myself talk. I can't hear myself think. I cannot remember from one minute to the next.

Why do I always have to tell you again and again?

Give me a minute to think. Just let me catch my breath.

Don't you ever stop to ask?

I'm going to tell you something. I'm going to give you the benefit of my advice. Do you want some good advice?

You think the sun rises and sets on you, don't you? You should get down on your hands and knees and thank God. You should count your blessings. Why don't you look around yourself and really see yourself for once, just for once in your life? You just don't know when you're well off. You have no idea how the rest of the world lives. You are as innocent as the day you were born. You should thank your lucky stars. You should try to make amends. You should do your best to put it all out of your mind. Worry never got anybody anywhere. Whatever you do, promise me this—keep an open mind. What do I say to you, where do I start with you, how do I make myself heard with you? I don't know where to begin with you, I don't know where to start with you, I don't know how to impress upon you the importance of every single solitary word. Thank God I am alive to tell you, thank God I am here to tell you, thank God you've got someone to tell you, I only wish I could begin to tell you, if there were only some way someone could tell you, if only there were someone here to tell you, but you don't want to listen, you don't want to learn, you don't want to know, you don't want to help yourself, you just want to have it all your own sweet way and go on as if nothing has changed. Who can talk to you? Can anyone talk to you? You don't want anyone to talk to you. So far as you are concerned, the whole world could drop dead.

You think death is a picnic? Death is no picnic. Face facts, don't kid yourself, people are trying to talk some sense into you, it's not all just fun and fancy free, it's not all just high, wide, and handsome, it's not all just make-believe.

You take the cake, you take my breath away—you are really one for the books. Be smart and play it down. Be smart and stay in the wings. Be smart and let somebody else carry the ball for a change.

You know what I've got to do? I've got to talk like a Dutch uncle to you.

I've got to handle you with kid gloves.

Let me tell you something no one else would have the heart

to tell you. Look far and wide—because they are few and far between! Go ahead, go to the ends of the earth, go to the highest mountain, go to any lengths, because they won't lift a finger for you—or didn't you know that some things are not for man to know, that some things are better left unsaid, that some things you shouldn't wish on a dog, not on a bet, not on your life, not ever at all?

What do you want? You want the whole world to revolve around you, you want the whole world at your beck and call? That's what you want, isn't it? Be honest with me.

Answer me this one question.

How can you look me in the face?

Don't you dare act as if you didn't hear me. You want to know what's wrong with you? This is what is wrong with you. You are going to the dogs, you are lying down with dogs, you are waking sleeping dogs—don't you know enough to go home before the last dog is dead?

When are you going to learn to leave well enough alone?

You know what you are?

Let me tell you what you are.

You are betwixt and between.

I'm on to you, I've got your number, I can see right through you—I warn you, don't you dare try to put anything over on me or get on my good side or lead me a merry chase.

So who's going to do your dirty work for you now?

Do me a favor and don't make me laugh!

Oh, sure, you think you can rise above it, you think you can live all your life with your head in the clouds in a cave like a hermit, without rhyme or reason, without a hitch, without batting an eyelash, without a leg to stand on, without a little bit of butter on your bread, but let me tell you something—you're all wet! You know what? You're trying to get away with false pretenses, that's what! But you know what is wrong with you? Because I am here to tell you what is wrong with you. There is no happy medium with you, there is no live and let live with you, there is no by the same token with you, because talking to you is like talking to a brick wall to you!

Pay attention to me!

You think I am talking just to hear myself talk?

# PRAISE

# JABES!—AND

# MYRON COHEN

———

HOW ABOUT A JOKE? I really tell a really great joke. And I really tell a really great one as great as it can be told. Or is it greatly? Anyway, this is the only thing I think I can do in public anymore—tell people a joke. You I am going to tell a joke to—because look how much in the public you are. Well, you may think otherwise, you may have other ideas otherwise, but what's the diff, everybody's ideas?

It's a pool.

There's a pool.

There's, you know, there's Mrs. Feigenbaum, there is the widow Feigenbaum, and she sees this person sitting there, and so she says to him, Mrs. Feigenbaum says to him, "So look at you, sitting there all by yourself in the sun like this, so pale, so pale, a man so pale. So tell me," Mrs. Feigenbaum says, "so what is your name, pray tell?"

"Schmulevitz," says the man.

"That's nice, that's nice," says Mrs. Feigenbaum. "But so

listen," says Mrs. Feigenbaum, "so how come a nice gentleman such as yourself comes out here to the pool so pale? So you must have a wonderful business, never to get one single instant for you to go out in the sun outside."

"Nah," says Schmulevitz, "it wasn't a business, it's not a business—it's jail, it's instead I just got out of jail."

"Jail?" says Mrs. Feigenbaum. "You just got out of jail?" says Mrs. Feigenbaum. "So it's probably," Mrs. Feigenbaum says, "it's probably you were making a lot of money and so why give it all to the government? So is it such a crime, getting a little too cute with the taxes and so forth?"

"Nah," says Schmulevitz. "It was murder," says Schmulevitz. "I killed somebody," says Schmulevitz.

"So you say you killed somebody?" says Mrs. Feigenbaum. "Well, sure," Mrs. Feigenbaum says, "you were probably on your way home from your office with all the cash and there's these robbers which come to get your cash from you, so what could you do, what could anybody do, didn't you have to take the bull by the horns?"

"Nah," says Schmulevitz, "it was my wife. I killed my wife."

"No kidding," says Mrs. Feigenbaum. "Your wife," says Mrs. Feigenbaum. "You killed your wife?" says Mrs. Feigenbaum. "But, look, the hussy was probably driving you crazy and making a sick man of you, constantly never putting a meal on the table, constantly always with the get me this, the get me that, running you ragged all over the place with the constant eating out every night and the constant dancing all of the time until dawn every night."

"Nah," says Schmulevitz, "she never asked for nothing. Meals, meals, this person in the kitchen was like an angel. What a wonderful creature," says Schmulevitz. "This was the world's most wonderful creature," says Schmulevitz. "Nobody ever had a better beloved creature," says Schmulevitz. "So like who could tell you like what gets into me, one minute this honey of a sweetie-pie is saying to me darling, darling, what a terrific husband you are, the next minute I am giving this woman such a smack with an axe."

"Oh," says Mrs. Feigenbaum. "Oh, so I see," says Mrs. Feigenbaum. "So listen," says Mrs. Feigenbaum, "so doesn't this mean you probably are like, you know, like a single fella, right?"

Okay, great or not?

So face it, so maybe not so great.

But pretty good, pretty darned good—or, anyhow, pretty goddamned good enough for the likes of you, pal—which is like somebody who can't even be one hundred percent honest about who is a riot and who's not.

# THE
# TRAITOR

———

THEY LOOKED TO ME to be Tibetan or Mongolian or—I
don't know, I just want to say it—Burmese. Oh, but this is
inexcusable. This is embarrassing. Really, there's not a blessed
thing I know about national types like those, about what they're
supposed to look like or what you'd call them if you knew. I
mean, maybe this couple had actually looked to me mostly like
they came from Thailand, but I didn't know how to say it, so I
right away gave up on the likelihood because I could see ahead,
see the situation of the adjective coming, and knew it would
have me stumped frontwards, backwards, and sideways, knew it
would have had me whipped hands-down. Thailander? Thailander can't be right. At least I would not bank on my ever having
heard anyone say it—say Thailander. Great day, you'd know it if
you'd ever heard anyone say it. But neither can I imagine what
you might alternatively say, unless it's Thai*land*ian, which, now
that I have actually said it, sounds to me excessively improbable
and possibly insulting.

You may as well know that I once got into some absolutely

hopeless trouble over a thing like that—from referring to a certain person by this name rather than by that name. Or it may have been the other way around. Frankly, it was not all that long ago, this misunderstanding. It remains to be proved, in fact, which, if either, was the case—that I misunderstood or was misunderstood. Not that the couple on the subway represented the opportunity for the same sort of confusion. Oh, no, theirs was a confusion of an entirely different sort. I mean, you could see that they were not the kind of people to care a fig for how anyone anywhere might elect to propose a category for them. Or do I mean something simpler and can't say it? But I am a man of action, you see, and not, as you will also see, of words. Although I doubtlessly know more about words than would most persons operating along the lines of the job title of my ilk.

Dropped a stitch back there. Had meant to say that these two—the man and the woman—looked to me as if they had reached what is sometimes called "a higher state."

To be absolutely candid with you, I just don't know how I got us into this Thailand thing. Actually, the more I let thought attack the question, the more I am willing to favor the notion that they, the couple, were very likely Siberian, by which I mean the man and woman who were sitting across from me on the subway last week. Ah, but I forget, I forget—so bundled up against the cold they were, not on your life could they really have been Siberian. Unless, of course, I am making the mistake of believing that where you come from has something visibly to do with how you react to what the temperature is where you go to. On the other hand, who is to say one hasn't come to us from Siberian parentage yet was nonetheless native to somewhere else where one might grow up warm?

Except they didn't look that way. Not to me, at least. To me, they looked like people who had gotten used to living in measureless wretchedness and then unused to it. You know what they looked like to me? They looked like people who were freezing in New York.

But you must know how everyone will look just this very way to you when you see them on the subway and it is winter in New York. Think of books nobody ever really reads but which by our age who cares if they catch you at it. At not having read them, I mean. Me, too, I didn't read those free-thinking ones, either.

Siberia. I take it back—what could I know about Siberia?

Didn't I say they were sitting right across from me? Because it was actually at a little angle from me that they were sitting— since these were the days when a subway car on the Lexington line had at one end two two-seater affairs that were not exactly opposite of each other but were sort of off from each other at a little slant. Anyhow, the picture I'm trying to get painted, it's them on one side and it's me on the other, whereas as for the rest of the car—believe it or not—this is not every day, I don't have to tell you—its empty, empty, empty, not one other—hey!— dead soul sitting or standing.

Can you beat it? From when they get on at Eighty-sixth Street to when she got off without him at Forty-second, there is nobody in this subway car but I and they. Or is it them and me?

Now *there* is the whole point of my telling you all of this in the first place, which is that *they*, the couple, didn't. I mean, get off the train in each other's company. And not only that, but *this*—which is that *he*, the Siberian fellow, he tricked her into it—actually faked her out, by hook and by crook got her onto the platform and then cut back into the car without her.

No, I'm not doing this anywhere near right. I'm talking and I'm talking—but you do not know what on earth is going on, and couldn't possibly.

I am starting again.

Here is the whole thing from the start again.

I said they got on at Eighty-sixth?

No, no, it is I that gets on at Eighty-sixth!

That is my practice—get on where I have to get on—the Lexington line, the Broadway line, here, there, everywhere in the city. But what should instantly give me away to you the morning I am reporting on to you is that it is swept clean of people, the car that I get aboard on—except for them, of course—if they, the couple, were in fact already on it—the Siberians, the Thailanders, the Mongolians—you know, the whatever—huddled together in one of the two-seater affairs at one end of the car—a man and a woman—this is guesswork, of course—who I am guessing must be in their seventies at least—just little disks of faces to guess from, that's how hooded they were with scarves and caps, with weird coverings. So it is not just the eyes that give me the Asian notion, not just the bones around the eyes, but also the bandaged effect that gets imparted to the head when these people are seeking ceremony or protection from the weather. No, that's off—that does not make any sense, does it?

Oh, Lord, I am really getting out of my depth with this. It's just that you turn on the television and what do you see but Tokyo, Seoul, whole columns of them shoulder-to-shoulder, kids, endless legions of kids, always up in fucking arms over this, that, or the other thing, their noggins all done up with this ad-hoc crap on them, the whole street chuggyjammed with them doing this slow, scary sort of creepy Bangkokian jog shit.

So that's why I almost thought that, actually. Namely, almost thought that they might both be Cong or Jap, except that he was such a tall bugger, six-three, if I am any judge, whereas she was a good one, too—the old woman, I mean—every inch of her as tall as she had to be, and maybe then some on top of it. Not that I ever was standing when either of them was. Not that any of what I am saying to you is anything but a guess. But you couldn't have thought about it anymore than I was thinking about it, even saying to myself, "Make up your mind," meaning, that I should make up my mind what kind of height I was involved with because I already knew I might want to later on get some writing out of it—a report, at least—and now look, this is just what I am doing, aren't I?—sitting there and getting debriefed. But so what if she wasn't, and he wasn't, either? I mean, even if the both of them put together weren't enough to make up even one short human being, does this mean I have to go to bed without any supper?

It is not out of the question, the truth.

Wasn't there something somewhere in my reading, something I read somewhere where there is this region of the Orient where the people are positively tremendous?

But maybe I didn't read it. Maybe it was in a movie when it was raining and the whole school had to stay inside and couldn't have recess. You know, the climate and the crops and the trade routes of somewhere, and the enormous size of certain of its citizens. Or maybe we were doing a class project on cotton, and it was also the year of the adjective.

Which reminds me to tell you that I am not dumb. I promise you, I am more than competent in speaking to the distinction between that which is only morphologically adjectival and that which is instead, or as well, syntactically thus.

Unless you forgot. I mean, about back there where I was giving the appearance of being flummoxed as to what you transmute Thailand to when you want to say, "I think that they both were . . ."

Wait. When you say, "The man was Mongolian," you replicate the morphology but not the function that is exhibited in "The man was a Mongolian."

But I imagine you have gone and forgotten all this. Ah, God, one offers speculations and, once one has them out on offer, forgets.

Sorry.

Really.

Been farting around for altogether too long now. You've got me dead to rights—just another man of action knocking his fnocking brains out to come across as a man of thought.

Meant *transform*, not *transmute*.

It's so hard.

You shouldn't have to know anything to do something. I mean, it doesn't seem fair, does it? But that's how the setup is: know-how, smarts, skilled labor—fellows like me, nothing uncalled-for, nothing spontaneous. Ah, it's all such a lousy deal, start off with things which couldn't be simpler, and before you know it, what?

The answer is that you're struggling against great torrents of shit, complexities you never had the brains to create. Thought you were just doing arithmetic, yes? Whereas, Jesus, if you're not Boltzmann, you might as well give up, go fishing, work for the F.B.I. instead, be an idiot.

I saw them.

The car was empty.

I tell you, it was the coldest of damnable days! It was New York and I was freezing—and them, they—they looked so warm together—they looked like Eskimos together—the man and woman, they looked so comfy with each other, so used to, so hardened by, things.

Assuming.

Because how much could I actually see of them?

You realize I am sitting in the seat that is almost exactly facing theirs? I mean, I had to. I had the whole car to choose from, sure—but let us not forget my specialty, my assignment, the noun to know me by, why I was there, why I am here.

You'd look at me and see a fellow who doesn't look like anything—a big man in a big coat, lots of room for everything.

Oh, you bet, they could have been Eskimos.

They had to be something.

He kept scribbling things. He had in his pocket these folded-up papers and he kept getting them out and scribbling things on them—not words, of course, but numerals, I think, or symbols from sciences that we keep warning these people they have no effing business messing with. Equations, disequilibriums—things, didn't I say things? But, all right, this is not my element, and I would be the first to admit it.

On the other hand, just don't think I couldn't see him plain as day, the sonofabitch scratching away at these folded-up papers, the rat acting as if he were up to something big—reaching for some elusive result, putting on like some fucking Taiwani or something, like some Taiwanese whizbang, like some trafficker in new methodologies feeling his way by brainy frigging fingertip.

Oh, you know, you know—so absorbed he seemed, so thoroughly insulated, isolated—I don't know—innoculated from things, the old broad meanwhile nattering away at him, all jabber jabber without letup or surcease—get napkins, get ketchup,

aren't we all out of mayo? Or so I was made to speculate—
because who could fucking hear? And even if I could have,
wouldn't it've been in Singaporese?

Or what is it, Singapo?

Oh, yes, Dr. Wu, Dr. Wu—that's who's at the bottom of all
of this, bigshot sitting over there working out cosmological
models in exponents of ten, Mrs. Wu going on at him and on at
him, get this, Wen Lung, get that, Wen Lung, him looking like
he's not listening to the lyrics but only to the music—all out of
eggs, all out of bread, don't forget the eggs and bread!

I'll tell you the truth. It wasn't that many minutes between
the time I got on and he got her to get off, but it was enough of
them for me to make all of this up. You know, Dirac, Besso,
Lorentz, and good old Wen Lung Wu, the dirty turncoat hump-
ing it on down to the U.N. with whatever he's got going on
down there in the language of Hwei. Hey, and isn't this why the
car is empty of other riders? Isn't it because a hit has been set up
to cut the cocksucker off?

And doesn't Wennie know it, can't Wennie see it for himself,
can't the asshole put two and two together and get it that him
and her have been marked for death? That they will never make
it off this train in fewer than too many pieces? That somewhere
between here and Forty-second they are going to be gunned
down, eradicated, interdicted, bumped the fuck off? Or maybe
not until they get out and start running, screaming bloody-murder for the Free World and the Third World and the One World
to come save them . . . except how do you finish this, declarative

or interrogative? Well, it was all imperative the instant the loose-coated motherfucker had got himself all aboard, confederates having cleared the car, confederates having closed off escape, confederates having screwed down the hatches, having prepared all preparable matters, spot-cleaned the venue for the point-shooter, made way for the remover. So what, then, is left for it but for them to put the best face on it and huddle in some species of Asian-ish cuddle?

Ah, Christ, I hear her say, "Clorox, get Clorox, don't forget, make a note," and him, he writes $OQ^2 = t^2x^2 - y^2yz^2$ and thinks, "Goodbye, my love—goodbye!"

But as I already told you, the old fraud faked her out at Forty-second. I mean, if he had meant to get rid of her, that's just what he did—got her off without him, got her good and off.

Oh, the old sly-sides!

I tell you, these people with their eyes, they are not for one instant to be trusted. Why, the rascal, he leapt up with a great start as we drew into the station—fairly leapt, or leaped, I say—as if to say, "Good heavens, Mrs. Wu—your hubby appears to have been incalculably distracted—preoccupied beyond all fathom-ing—mercy sakes, dear lady, darned near made us miss our sta-tion—let us hasten, sweet wife, let us take ourselves away."

Oh, the dickens, the dirty dickens!

Imagine this. See it as I, your patriot, saw it—the old repro-bate flinging himself at the doors and she, the poor dear, stagger-ing after—so completely bewildered, taken so completely unawares—plunging blindly after, bad on her ancient feet, blisters bleeding, I don't doubt, corns, spurs, calluses, great horny bunions—totally but totally disoriented, not to mention so helplessly overcome by an absolute riot of agonies—but nevertheless making her way just well enough, gaining on her hubby just barely, while he, the fnocking four-flusher, he executes the adroitest of pivots—and all with such gallantry, the very sheerest of chivalries, as in "Ladies first, ladies first—my very dearest lady of the realm."

Well, you know what I say?

I say, "Radies first."

*Radies, radies, radies*—her on the platform, him still with me on the train, the whole shebang moving again, hell-bent for Thirty-third.

"Lealm." That's what the dirty prick said!

But to be absolutely evenhanded, I'll say this for him—which is that the bum actually winked at me once the doors had shut her away from me and we were off and clattering along on our deadly way again. By God, the bum, he was sitting back down in the same seat when he let me have it—nicked his eye at me, like gunfire, just the once—pow! Then took out his folded-up papers, his little stub of a pencil, making, for my money, a great Jew-y show of the thing, the filthy fucking Chink.

Oh, let's not beat around the bush, the yig was *Writing Secret Stuff*—isn't it high time everybody just quit all the shit and said what he means?

But here's the thing, which *was* he, doing what he did—dirty traitor or dirty savior?

Because you can see how it could go either way, answer either claim.

At any rate, it was a local, as I said. Or if I didn't say it—hadn't!—then I just did.

Forget it.

What we had to work with was its being Thirty-third next. This means—go ahead and count them for yourself—nine numbers to get the Euher out and get the Thompson on, nine numbers to get the Thompson on and shoot once, nine numbers to shoot once and get the Thompson off, nine numbers to do what everybody is waiting for you to do and get everything back in under your coat.

Which is big and loose.

Adjectives—oh, Christ!

# BEHOLD THE INCREDIBLE REVENGE OF THE SHIFTED P.O.V.

―――――――――

How shall we say the clock was bought and paid for? For surely the seller's sticker on the thing declared a figure remarkably bolder than these youngsters could decently manage. But they were so keen, the two of them, and so ungovernable in their zeal. Of what earthly pertinence was it that their purse could scarce stand up to the mild demands of the humblest item in this shop? And the clock, oh my, as to its forbidding tariff, great heavens, this, please be clear, was certain to be seen by most shoppers as another, and much harsher, matter entirely. But what, please be, did other matters, certain or otherwise, have to do with anything when it was naught but the pressure of necessity itself that rested its infinite weight on the possessed hearts of these young people? For there the clock stood in its stony oaken case, all solemnity in its olden bearing (after all, the sticker stated "Early Nineteenth Century" no less forthrightly than it stated the price) as it spoke its artful speech of sturdiness, of continuity, of permanence, offering to deliver these affiliations first and therefore, when the time was right, everything else.

It said it could confer on them as much.

Or so we heard it pledge its word to the new homemakers.

"Wow, that's no joke!" the boy announced with some excessive gusto, meaning to exaggerate his astonishment not just for the good fun of making fun of himself but also to suggest to the shop's proprietor—who had hovered into position—that, in fact, for these two customers, the amount would be no large sum at all.

"But only think of it!" the girl exclaimed. "I mean, wouldn't it be like an heirloom really? I mean, when we have a family, couldn't we just sort of pass it on to them the way real people do, sort of like generations upon generations forever?"

The boy colored at his spouse's high sentence, wanting to hurry to correct her where it had struck his ear that the girl had gone with it, great Christ, a measure or two too far. But the boy knew the damage had been done, that it was always already centuries too late ever to withdraw the smallest wrongness, that the proprietor—the man hovering ever more tellingly into position—a lofty enough presence to hover, actually—had heard all, judged all—"generations upon generations forever" indeed!—doubtlessly savoring the evidence on a tongue that would publish conclusions elsewhere.

Ah, God, the boy could hear the verdict carrying down the ages after him: "Innocent young dear has gone and got itself a goodish burden, now hasn't it? Dreadful silly sap."

That did it, or so it seems not unsafe for us to suppose.

At any rate, grinning horribly, the boy motioned for the girl to fetch the "family" checkbook from her handbag—so that, by whatever means fiscal, the clock was got—and a note was accordingly made and thereafter wired to the fancy key that poked from the fancy keyhole whose lock could let you get at the lordly pendulum either for the business of starting it up or, if ever required, shutting it down.

Sold.

And so forth and so on.

We are reporting the clock was theirs.

A "grandmother clock" was what status the clock was rendered by the reference books in which its kind was pictured, this, it is not unlikely, in pursuit of a program to restrict the thing to a rank not so grand at all—and though the provenance of the clock was very probably more local than not, still (the seller had seemed so tall, so hovering, so . . . *otherly*), once the clock had taken up its post against their bedroom wall (there was really nowhere else for them to fit their purchase, what with the premises being—the marriage was hardly yet out of its cradle— so cruelly unbaronial), the owners succumbed to the practice of engaging the phrase "our imported piece" whenever inquiries were made by one or another young couple who, after very persuasive fare indeed, at the card table set up for the purpose in the kitchen, were escorted back into the bedroom for a bit of TV with coffee and dessert and cordials.

"Oh, but it's so unutterably special," the other wife would say. "No wonder you want it back here where you sleep, where a chic antique of its type can really be better appreciated on a much more frequent basis."

"Yeah, nice," the other husband would say. "So you guys inherit it from your families or something?"

But whatever enthusiasms the other young couple would insert into the ethers as they bit into cake and drank from goblets and sipped from cups no bigger than big thimbles, sooner or later someone would be bound to observe—generally when the clock's imperturbable chimes were finally being heard from—that the time was the better part of an hour fast.

Or slow.

But wrong.

Fast or slow but wrong.

Always wrong.

Never not anything but chaotically wrong.

Off.

Way off.

Not right.

Not once.

Nowhere even close.


There was no remedy for it.

Years into the marriage, the thing still tolled the hour nowhere near the hour—and when one went to the living room (oh, as they will to all couples who accomplish the early stewardship of a magisterial object, other important objects had issued to our couple, even a commodious enough living room had) to see what time it was, one had to smack one's head and reinstruct oneself that for such a use, for telling the time, the clock was no good at all. Whereupon, whichever of them it was, that party would then get himself prayerfully down onto his knees, would work the fancy key, would draw open the panel whose business it was to keep from view the relentless commerce of the pendulum, would put a finger out to stop it, would then reset the whole affair, hideously mindful all the while that whatever adjustment was being made will have long since, hours hence, begun to yield to the mischief transferring exacting correction into more and more violent error.

The bother was pointless.

Clock people were summoned from other counties, from distant precincts, from bizarre neighborhoods, wild sullen grisly creatures, who, angerly bearded and extravagantly undeterred, brought with them impossibly exotic instruments and, sometimes, wordless ghostly staring children, their fathers keeping to their dismal labors for days without sleep, taking no recesses for food even—greasy oblongs of oil-dark canvas spread out all about as the place more and more accumulated the parts of . . . *our imported piece*!—the thing nauseatingly sundered, undone, suddenly truly charmlessly alien, whatever the truth of its origin.

No help.

Nothing worked.

The clock kept keeping the wrong time.

But no one is saying that it was ever a stroke less reassuring to look upon.

He who looked upon the clock was reassured.

She, too.

Made present to the sacrament of things going on, of no change, of the venerable further venerating itself.

It was okay.


The children had come and gone.

To be sure, the notion of the generations was just beginning to exert itself good and proper the year the couple packed up and gave up the place where the marriage had conducted its offspring into the habits that had been proclaimed for them. So here was the time for something smaller and more manageable, for a dwelling better fitted to the compressions of middle age—and the clock, of course, went to that dwelling with them—all the time in the world for passing such a patrimony along to the first one to wed—no, to the first one to honor the ceremonies of homemaking—oh, but no yet again—to the first one to express the resolution to prostrate himself and spouse before a token of the household, consenting to welcome the instruction the clock could give.

But, look, see how we, the tellers of what is told, are not exempt from what is said?

Behold, must not the clock keep perfect time before the story can be a story?

And so it does!

All day.

Every day.

And all the next ones, too.

Magic.

How else to explain?

The spontaneous institution of what was wanted—everything in unimprovable order—nothing even a tick's tock off.

Go ahead, call the time-keepers, get in touch with the lucky custodians, telephone from right in there—we mean from right in there in the little sleeping room the widow and I have now taken to storing the clock in and to keeping tidied and readied for the visits of our children's children's children.

You'll see.

Say, "Could you please tell me what time it is, please?"

Now watch the clock.

Right on the money, yes?

But here is the thing.

Every time the old woman and I hear it chiming the time it really is, a ridiculous condition of panic takes up our minds in its hands and twists. I mean, the clock, the good old clock—our very index of the durable order of things—has got us scared stiff.

# WEIGHT

———

THE FOUR THINGS are a key, two benches, and a bicycle wrapped in party paper but not where the handgrips and the foot-pedals are.

The key opens someone else's door.

The park bench looks out on a river.

The other bench is down where the subway runs.

The bicycle's a chimpanzee's.

The key is a duplicate.

The park bench stands in sunlight.

Four citizens are seated on the bench down here. The one free place is next to me.

The chimpanzee will speak for himself. But I say it's custom-made, the bicycle, balanced to the gram. See where the paper's split? That's chromium underneath.

The key is cut from cheap metal, a feathery replica of the brass original—lent, copied, seventy-five cents. It has no weight worth notice. Sometimes he does not know it's in his pocket. But it's there sometimes—once a week.

Of course, it's filthy down there, but it's also filthy up here. And the floor the chimpanzee rides on, this is filthy too—peanut shells, popcorn, gummy substances flattened out to ovals, a law of physics, the law of shapes.

"I started on the bicycle when I was half the size you see. It's adjustable, wing nuts for all the crucial parts. I did not have the hat at first. But after one circle without a slipup, I did. After four, the jacket. After eight, the trousers. When I could keep it up and keep it up—the shoes were what I got for it. They're sturdy. They're black. See the buckles for getting them on and off?"

Now for people.

There's the man in such a hurry, hand in pocket, wristwatch raised to read the time. There's the couple in the park, the slowest pace of all, the bench they're oh so slowly making for. There's the woman down here marching back and forth. She reaches her mark, shouts, "Leather from Morocco!" turns about, marches again, marching back and forth.

You don't want to see her. I try not to. They try not to, the others on this bench. We are just passengers, persons waiting to be passengers. Oh, we really cannot wait to be. Will your train come before she does?

The old woman has the old man by the arm, to hold him up and steer. That's where they are going—to the bench in sunlight, to sit, to see the water—and the going is immense.

The man runs now, runs the last little bit, then puts his shoulders into it as he hustles up the five flights of stairs. He takes his hand out. He takes the key out.

The marching woman shouts, "Handbags! Beaded handbags!" But there is nothing in her hands.

Oh, God, don't let her jump, not while I'm still here. Oh, God, don't let her think to sit, not while I am here.

Sit.

Is there anything else that this man wants?

It's been too long from the bed to the bench—and he is not there yet. "Up, my darling," she must have said. "Such a lovely sunny day calling such a lovely boy."

Oh, yes, this is how she, this woman, would talk.

"Up, sweet love," she must have said. "Come, my beloved, another look."

It must have taken hours to get him dressed. See how nothing matches? Oh, it must have hurt to have the clothes go on—in something, touching anything, living one more minute.

He has his clothes off. He tunes the radio. Goes away, comes back, retunes. He looks at the clock, looks again, puts his hand in a trouser pocket, takes out his wristwatch. He's learned—always take your watch off.

"I learned without the paper on. The paper's just for show. What isn't? I learned. They put you on, you go. Listen, I can go and go. But I don't have to. An even dozen is all I ever have to. The bolero and knickers, they're satin, they're turquoise. See the pink piping? I had to wait and wait for the shoes. But I could have mastered the pedals with them. Cut off my feet, I still could have. The hat? It's red. That's traditional. Black, turquoise, pink, red—some ensemble, Jesus."

I looked. Or one of them looked. It only took one look and here she comes!

Oh, Jesus!

Should I check my watch and get up? Perhaps I must hasten to an engagement farther up the platform. But I am just sitting here, and now so is she.

Her beauty is impossible—oh, the back of her as she turns him by such considerate degrees.

"Sit, my love," she says.

He says, "You, dear—you sit first."

But I cannot really hear them speak.

When she sits, she is not crazy anymore. She sits primly, ru-ined ankles primly crossed. She breathes a small sigh and falls silent, just another citizen, speechless like us all.

He flexes the fingers on this hand, then on that hand, then all the toes. He looks at the clock, at the door, at the clock, at his clothes. There they are, all laid out for him to put back on—his turquoise knickers, his fine fitted jacket, his shoes.

But why bother with it all? Just the trousers, then—then open the door and run take a look.

"Buckle this side, buckle that side—even a horse could do it if he had a thumb. But the children shriek their approval. Yes, they like the buckling of the shoes better than the bicycling. Yes, yes, the leather hurts. But what doesn't?"

No, she is not waiting for a train. This is where she is when she sits. Yes, it is because she has kept him waiting longer than she has ever kept him waiting, longer than any of them ever did. Oh, it is because she has never kept him waiting that he runs down to take a look. Is the buzzer broken? Does she stand there, five flights down, calling him and calling him and he is way up here? She stands there, nodding, pleading, saying, "Please, my beloved, sit now—please, just sit." Look at his fingers flexing. Oh, God, he hurts! Oh, God, she's going to get up—and do what? Jump? Just march? Five flights half-undressed? Is there nothing he won't do? "I can do anything if you make me." But no one is waiting, no one is calling, no one is saying, "My beloved, my darling—my sweet, sweet love." She's marching, just marching. "Why must they be children? How can children know what it takes to do this? Can children ever know what it costs to keep your balance? They think everything does—houses stuck on mountain peaks of crayon going up." "Leather from Morocco!" Just march, don't jump! Back up the stairs, begging God, the slowest pace of all. "No, sweet love, first you—sit, please sit," and so she does. She sits and says, "Now you, my love," and guides him down. He stands there at that door. Nothing in this side, nothing in that side, nothing in the whole wide world. "There are no pockets in my trousers. If there were, I would load them down. Put rocks in, put people in, just to show them what I could carry and still go on and on." He turns and turns, these mute rotations—shirt, shoes, fine little jerkin all locked up inside.

I never had that duplicate.

Or a bicycle that fit my size.

Or the courage to stay seated when here comes the worst.

I have a wife. I have the ungainly weight of my love for her. I am the beast who can circle without letup. In theory. So far.

# HOW TO

# WRITE A POEM

---

I TELL YOU, I am no more a sucker for this thing of poetry
than the next fellow is. I mean, I can take it or leave it—a
certain stewarded pressure, some modulated pissing and moan-
ing, the practiced claims of a seasonal heart. But once in a blue
moon I have in hand a poem whose small unfolding holds me to
its period. It needn't be any great shakes, such a poem. I don't
care two pins for what its quality is. Christ, no—literature's not
what I look to poetry for.

Fear is.

You know—like the fear of nothing there.

You keep your head on straight, there'll be this breeze you'll
start to feel, a sort of dainty susurration of the words. That's
when you can bet the poor sap's seen it coming at him—an ordinary universe, the itemless clutter of an unmysterious world.
First chance he gets, it's a whole new ballgame, touching bases
while he races home free, that little telltale wind on the page
you're looking at as the gutless poet starts to work up speed.

Maybe I don't like poets—or people. But I just love to catch

some bardness at it, and then to test myself against the thingless-
ness that made him cut and run. What I do is I pick it up where
the old versner's nerve dumped him, right there where he just
couldn't stand to see where there's never going to be anything
where something never was.

It's no big deal. You just face down what he, in his chicken-
heart, couldn't. Then you type your version up and sign your
name to it. Next thing you do is get it printed as your own, sit
back and listen to them call you the real thing when you weren't.

It's the safest theft, a stolen poem—and who, tell me, doesn't
steal something? Besides, show me what a poet dares demand his
right to. A public reading? Public subsidy? But certainly not a
grand banality. Least of all the very one his cowardice dishon-
ored! Forget it—this is a person who is afraid.

What brings me to these brusque disclosures is an experience of
recent vintage, a poem I took over from some woman you'll
never hear of, and that I have since passed off—not without
applause—as my own.

Nothing to it.

Just you watch.

The text—I mean the one that came before me—situates us
in a situation as follows: two women, the poet and a widow, the
bereaved missus of the lover of the poet.

For how long had the lovers been lovers?

Long enough.

And the deceased deceased?

A less long time than that.

Whatever the precise relativities, we are talking about an adulterous liaison along the usual lines.

So far, so good—the loved and the loveless.

Of course, the poet is herself married. But since her spouse never enters the poem by more than intimation, we are led, I think, to conclude that his relation to all this is of no concern and of less importance. I mean, insofar as people going and fucking whom they weren't supposed to, the poet's spouse doesn't figure into any of this at all. He is not contingent, that is—at least not with respect to the prospect of what we are guessing must be coming.

Not so the dead man's wife. What I am suggesting is—what is suggested by the poet in the poem (oh yes, the poet, as I said, is *in* the poem, in the poem speaking)—is that an air of discovery thickens over things very greatly: the unsuspecting widow, her husband's sneaky copulations. But, naturally, this is where we are headed, where the original text is taking us—toward exposure, toward widow-know-all.

As for the one party the poem pays no mind to (now that the poet's version has been published—in not nearly so distinguished a setting as mine was), doesn't he, must not he, know all too, even as I write this?

But perhaps the spouses of poets don't read poetry.

Is this why the poet was in this fix in the first place.

What does it matter one way or the other, the poet's hubby, what he knows or what he doesn't? It's plain we're not required to direct toward him more than passing notice. The poet urges us to do as much. Or is it as little?

One dismissive reference.

What happens is this.

In the poem, remember?

We see the poet and the widow at the widow's. Newly back from the cemetery? We're not informed. Just this—a blustery day, late autumn, late morning, the women in pullovers and cardigans, grays, tans, tweeds, second sweaters arranged autumnishly over shoulders, legs brought back under buttocks.

A living room, a fire.

Are the principals seated on the floor?

I think so. I like to think so.

What we're told is the poet's here to lend a hand—help sort the dead man's papers, be good company, a goodly solace, a presence in an empty house. So we see the women being women together, being the bereaved together, fingering what the dead man wrote.

(Was he a poet, too? More than likely. Nowadays, there are many, many poets.)

We see them grieving lightly, smoothing skirts, reminiscing, sipping tea, making tidy. Well, we hear this, see that—I don't recollect if the poet really keeps her senses keyed to this or that event. So we see or hear their speeches when they reach into a carton to read aloud a bit of this, a bit of that.

You know—fellowship, fellowing. A little weeping. Women's shoulders, women's sweaters.

Nice.

When—didn't I say you'd guess it?—there's the wife with her hand at the bottom of a carton, and then her hand up and out, a neat packet in it, envelopes, a certain shape and paper, a certain fragrance, the dead man's record of the poet's indiscretion—letters that record copulations, letters that give account.

My God!

Etc., etc., etc.

But let's not be non-poets here. It's not as bad as all that. After all, the man's dead and buried. Quite beyond a scolding. The widow's seen plenty. The poet is a poet. Life is . . . life.

Oh, well.

So there we are (at the poet's placing), watching women being wiser together—cry a little, laugh a little, and then at last, seeing them, as the worldly will, embracing.

I'm not so sure who speaks first, nor what the poet said was said—the poet's poem being somewhere here among my trophies, but I being too caught up in this to get up to go check. Let's just say the widow says, "All these years, all these years, and who was he? He was who you talked to in these letters."

And the poet?

Who remembers?

But I expect she says whatever's said to someone being spacious for your benefit. Perhaps this: "No, no—it was you who had the better of it—the husband, the man."

Etc., etc.

The deceased, in pursuit of this assertion, is then celebrated, in two deft lines, for his performance in the two domains indicated.

Is there guile in this? Does the poet mean for us to take a tiny signal? Consider—why the symmetry? Is this the actual or the artful? And consider even further: Is there ever any difference?

Anyway, who's the kidder here—the poet in the poem or the poet not in it?

Balance, don't I detest it! A disproportion, there's the thing.

So there they are, poet and widow, usurper and usurped. Unclothed, as it were, disrobed—each jumpy to reach out and grab what's nearest for cover.

So they hurry to hide themselves in other people's bodies.

Another embrace. Sort of sisterly. Sisterly hugging. But it goes from this to carnal. At which point, the poem has furnished us with the great fraction of its text, the day (get this!) having, in its pliant time, accomplished (the poet tells us) a like progress.

So it's dusk when the two women make their way to bed, to do what the poet then gives us to imagine. But before we know it, the poet reappears, having projected (she explains) her astral body back to the room where she'd left us. We see, via her sight, the letters lying strewn among the papers. We see teacups, saucers, purses, shoes, sweaters. We see these things as things at first, as enumerations on the widow's Chinese rug.

The rest of the poem?

Now here you have it! For the poem now labors to extract

from the figure of these particulars a facsimile of the human spectacle, something serviceable in the way of a teaching, the event freed of the uneventful, the meaningless made to make way for meaning.

This was the poem the poet published and that I—genius that I am for spotting where a work has turned away from the unendurable vision it it—have since rewritten and passed along for a small disbursement and the fun.

Now let me tell you what I did.

In my poem, nothing's different. Word for word, it's all the same—up until the astral body comes back for a summary. Just like the fake poet, I take a look around. I see the same junk the poet saw. But in my poem, where I see them is on a decent grade of wall-to-wall broadloom bought at the mall and installed when rhyme—sorry, acquired when the price!—was right.

Now you know what art is.

And, notice, was I ever even once a person in that house?

Skip it.

It's all the same to me—the goddamn fancy phony rug, what's on it and its fucking whereabouts.

# UPON THE
# DOORSTEP OF
# THY HOUSE

---

WHAT are you looking at this for? Is there something you expect to derive from looking at this? What is it you expect to derive from looking at this? What result is it that you anticipate from the time that you give to this? What if it is not forthcoming? What if what you want from reading this is not forthcoming? Will you make it your business to assign blame if it is not forthcoming? Have you given any thought to the question of why it is you think something ought to be forthcoming? Do you not think it worth wondering why anyone should wish for anything to be forthcoming? Does it not occur to you that the wish for there to be something forthcoming subjects one to the allegation that one deems oneself to be incomplete, needful, deficient? Do you believe it inures to the grandeur of your notion of yourself to deem yourself any of the foregoing? Are you quite certain you quite positively know the sense in which the expression "inures to" is uttered? Is there not some particle of uncertainty somewhere in you? Is it not altogether too immediately

conceivable to you that you must have misconstrued the character of my meaning? Would it not at all give you to wonder for
you to come to discover you took a view of matters quite out of
keeping with what you were meant to? If someone says to you a
sentence wherein the device of "if not"—let alone "let alone"—
is in evidence, would you not feel yourself a dot unsteadier as
you went, if not disabled? Did the sentence just prior to this one
not warrant, as it went, my right to produce myself as your in-
quisitor? What is it in you that, despite every reason for you to be
rid of this exanimate exercise, animates you, keeps animating
you, will not quit animating you, to keep making you make
your way onward with such animal vivacity? Is this how you
have determined to un-determine yourself, how it is imagined
you will let alone yourself, how in a bounded event bondage, the
bondage, is a little like—you feel it!—infinitude?

# [ E N T I T L E D ]

————————

—WHEN did you first meet Gordon Lish?

—Nineteen thirty-four. In Hewlett, which is a place which is about twenty miles outside of New York City.

—Was there anything notable about him at the time? Did he strike you as in any wise out of the ordinary?

—No, not anything I can think of. But the conditions were special. There was a blizzard that day—the eleventh day of February, nineteen thirty-four. I know this seemed meaningful to the fellow, a sort of sign of sorts. For as long as I've known the man, he every so often speaks to what seems to him to be the significance of snowstorms in his life. You know, heavy snows showing up on his birthdays and the like.

—He is fascinated with himself.

—Oh, sure, but, you know, but who isn't?

—You kept in pretty close touch with Lish after that first touch with him?

—You bet. I thought he was tremendously good company, a placid chap and enormously sweet-natured. Oh, he was easy to be with, all right. Not much on his mind, but what little there was he'd share with you, no hesitation, not the least of it. Besides, it was never a problem keeping track of him. I mean, he stayed close to home back in those days—few friends, few outings, a dreamer chiefly. Guy could sit for hours just staring. It was pleasant. To tell you the truth, it was a comfort just to sit with him—restful, restorative. You know . . . certain persons give you certain feelings. Well, I liked him—I suppose this explains everything.

—He confided in you?

—Whatever was on his mind, sure. But as I've been trying to say, there wasn't much of it. He was . . . what did I say before— placid? He was like that—very placid, very passive—tranquil. Half-asleep, actually—sort of dozing.

—Happy?

—Oh, no question about it—the happiest!

—But then things changed. So far as you could see, what? What specifically?

—You mean the shift in him—from what he was in the old days to what he got to be as time wore on. Well, no telling. But I'm willing to give you my thoughts, which is that nothing changed in him exactly.

—You mean, things changed around him? The world went from one thing to another?

—No, no, not that. What I mean is that I don't think what happened to Lish was any different from what happens to anybody. I mean, it's not the world exactly—because the world just doesn't matter that much, if you know what I'm saying. Oh, heck, I'm getting all mixed up. Look, the thing is, it's got to do, I think, with time—with just the time and the time of it—witnessing, too much witnessing.

—Witnessing too much of the world?

—The other way around . . . the world witnessing too much of you. Or time doing it. I don't know.

—That doesn't make any sense.

—Well, as I said, it's one man's opinion.

—But you've stayed with him—kept your eye on him, at least—didn't, you know, turn a deaf ear to him.

—No doubt about it. And why not? The man still interests me more than anybody else does. The thing is, I've put a lot into the thing, don't forget.

—You see him every day?

—I'd get pretty funny-feeling if I didn't.

—Why so?

—Oh, you know how it is—for each of us, there's always going to be at least one person it just doesn't feel right being out of touch with.

—But what if Lish took himself out of touch with *you*?

—That's just exactly what I worry about.

—But what if he succeeds? What will happen if him and you, if that's it and that's it?

—You know, that's the very thing I've been telling the man day in and day out. I say to him, "Gordon, the day you look around and I'm not there for you to have me looking back, that's the day you're going to wish you were never born."

—And what does he say when this is what you say?

—Him? He says, "It snowed the day I was born. There was a blizzard the day I was born. It was the eleventh of February, nineteen thirty-four. It snowed like that on my thirteenth birth-day too. Both times, there were such big snowstorms. Both times, there was so much snow."